PENGUI

I9

THE WATER

AND OTHER STORIES

H. E. BATES

H. E. BATES

The Watercress Girl

AND OTHER STORIES

PENGUIN BOOKS

IN ASSOCIATION WITH
MICHAEL JOSEPH

Penguin Books Ltd, Harmondsworth, Middlesex
AUSTRALIA: Penguin Books Pty Ltd, 762 Whitehorse Road,
Mitcham, Victoria

—

First published by Michael Joseph 1959
Published in Penguin Books 1963

—

—

Made and printed in Great Britain
by Richard Clay & Company Ltd,
Bungay, Suffolk
Set in Monotype Garamond

Contents

The Cowslip Field   7

The Watercress Girl   16

Let's Play Soldiers   34

The Far Distant Journey   49

The Pemberton Thrush   59

Death and the Cherry Tree   73

A Great Day for Bonzo   83

The Butterfly   148

Love in a Wych Elm   157

The House with the Grape Vine 171

Great Uncle Crow   179

Source of the World   188

The Poison Ladies   198

The Cowslip Field

PACEY sat on the stile, swinging her legs and her cowslip-basket.

Pacey, he thought, was by far the littlest lady he had ever seen. She had very thick dumpy legs and black squashy button boots and a brown felt hat under which bright blue eyes roamed about like jellyfish behind large sun-shot spectacles. On her cheek, just under her right eye, was a big furry brown mole that looked like the top of a bulrush that had been cut off and stuck there.

Pacey was nice, though. He liked Pacey.

'How far is it now to the cowslip field, Pacey?' he said.

'A step or two furder yit,' Pacey said.

'It's not *furder*,' he said. 'It's *further*.'

'Oh! is't?' Pacey said. 'All right, it's *further*. I never knew such a boy for pickin' me up afore I'm down.'

'And it's not *afore*,' he said. 'It's *before*.'

'Oh! is't?' Pacey said. 'All right, *before* then. I never knowed sich a boy for whittlin' on me –'

'And it's not *on*,' he said. 'It's *of* –'

'Here,' Pacey said, 'for goodness' sake catch holt o' the cowslip-basket and let me git down and let's git on. Else we'll never be there afore bull's-noon.'

When Pacey jumped down from the stile her legs sank almost to the top of her button boots in meadow grasses. She was so thick and squatty that she looked like a duck waddling to find the path across the field.

7

In that field the sun lay hot on sheets of buttercups. Soon when he looked at Pacey's boots they were dusty yellow faces, with rows of funny grinning eyes. At the end of the field rolled long white hedges of hawthorn, thick and foamy as the breakers he had once seen at the seaside, and from a row of sharp green larches, farther on, he heard a cuckoo call.

It was past the time when the larches had little scarlet eye-lashes springing from their branches but he still remembered them.

'Pacey,' he said, 'why do the trees have –'

'Jist hark at that cuckoo,' Pacey said. 'Afore long it'll charm us all to death.'

'Pacey,' he said, 'why don't cowslips grow in this field?'

'Because it ain't a cowslip field,' Pacey said, 'don't you know that? Don't you know the difference between a cowslip field and a buttercup field? If you don't it's time you did. Now you jis run on and git to the next stile and sit there quiet and wait fer me.'

From the next stile he sat and watched Pacey waddling down the slope of the field, between dazzling sheets of buttercups, under a dazzling high blue sky. In the wide May morning she looked more than ever like a floundering little duck, funnier, tinier than ever.

'Pacey,' he said, 'will you ever grow any bigger?'

'Not unless me luck changes a lot more'n it's done up to yit.'

'Will I grow any bigger?'

''Course you will.'

'Well then, why won't you?'

'Hark at that cuckoo,' Pacey said. 'If it's called once this morning, it's called a thousand times.'

In the next field brown and white cows were grazing and Pacey took his hand. Some of the cows stood at a pond, over their hocks in water, flicking flies from their white-patched brown rumps in the sun. All across the field there were many ant-hills and Pacey let him run up and down them, as if they were switchbacks, always holding his hand.

Her own hands were rough and clammy and warm and he liked them.

'What do the ants do in their ant-hills all the time, Pacey?' he said.

'They git on with their work,' Pacey said, ''ithout chattering so much.'

As they passed the pond he could smell the thick warm odours of may-bloom and fresh dung that the cows had dropped and mud warming in the sun. All the smell of rising summer was in the air. The tips of a few bulrushes, so brown and so like Pacey's mole, were like the last tips of winter, half-strangled by rising reeds.

Then somehow he knew that the next field was the cow-slip field and he suddenly broke free of Pacey's hand and ran jumping over the last of the ant-hills until he stood on a small plank bridge that went over a narrow stream where brook-lime grew among bright eyes of wild forget-me-not.

'Pacey, Pacey, Pacey!' he started shouting. 'Pacey!'

He knew he had never seen, in all his life, so many cow-slips. They covered with their trembling orange heads all the earth between himself and the horizon. When a sudden

9

breeze caught them they ducked and darted very gently away from it and then blew gently back again.

'We'll never gather them all before it's dark, Pacey,' he said, 'will we?'

'Run and git as many as you can,' Pacey said. 'It won't be dark yit awhile.'

Running, he tripped and fell among cowslips. He did not bother to get to his feet but simply knelt there, in a cowslip forest, picking at the juicy stems. All the fragrance of the field blew down on him along a warm wind that floated past him to shake from larches and oaks and hedges of may-bloom a continuous belling fountain of cuckoo calls.

When he turned to look for Pacey she was on her knees, dumpier, squattier than ever, filling her hands with golden sheaves of flower.

'Pacey, what will we do with them all?' he said. 'What will we do with them all?'

'Mek wine,' Pacey said. 'And I wouldn't be surprised if it were a drop o' good.'

Soon he was running to Pacey with his own sheaves of flower, putting them into the big brown basket. Whenever he ran he buried his face in the heads of flower that were so rich and fragrant and tender. Then as he dropped them into the basket he could not resist dipping his hands into the growing mound of cowslips. They felt like little limp kid gloves. They were so many soft green and yellow fingers.

'The basket'll soon be full, Pacey,' he said. 'What will we do when the basket's full?'

'Put 'em in we hats,' Pacey said. 'Hang 'em round we necks or summat.'

'Like chains?'

'Chains if you like,' Pacey said.

Soon the basket was almost full and Pacey kept saying it was bloomin' hot work and that she could do with a wet and a wind. From a pocket in her skirt she took out a medicine bottle of milk and two cheese cakes and presently he and Pacey were sitting down in the sea of cowslips, resting in the sun.

'The basket's nearly full,' he said. 'Shall we start making chains?'

'There'll be no peace until you do, I warrant.'

'Shall we make one chain or two chains?'

'Two,' Pacey said. 'I'll mek a big 'un and you mek a little 'un.'

As he sat there threading the cowslip stalks one into another, making his chain, he continually looked up at Pacey, peering in her funny way, through her thick jelly spectacles, at her own cowslip chain. He noticed that she held the flowers very close to her eyes, only an inch or two away.

'Pacey,' he said, 'what makes the sky blue?'

'You git on with your chain,' Pacey said.

'Who put the sky there?'

'God did.'

'How does it stay up there?'

Pacey made a noise like a cat spitting and put a cowslip stalk into her mouth and sucked it as if it were cotton and she were threading a needle.

'How the 'nation can I thread this 'ere chain,' she said, 'if you keep a-iffin' and a-whyin' all the time?'

Squinting, she peered even more closely at her cowslips,

so that they were now almost at the end of her nose. Then he remembered that that was how she sang from her hymn-book on Sundays, in the front row of the choir. He remembered too how his mother always said that the ladies in the front row of the choir sat there only to show off their hats and so that men could look at them.

'Have you got a young man, Pacey?' he said.

'Oh! dozens,' Pacey said. 'Scores.'

'Which one do you like best?'

'Oh! they're like plums on a tree,' Pacey said. 'So many I don't know which one on 'em to pick.'

'Will you get married, Pacey?'

Pacey sucked a cowslip stalk and threaded it through another.

'Oh! they all want to marry me,' Pacey said. 'All on 'em.'

'When will you?'

'This year, next year,' Pacey said. 'When I git enough plum-stones.'

'Why do you have to have plum-stones?'

'Oh! jist hark at that cuckoo all the time,' Pacey said. 'Charming us to death a'ready. How's your chain?'

His chain was not so long as Pacey's. She worked neatly and fast, in spite of her thick stumpy fingers. Her chain was as long as a necklace already, with the cowslips ruffled close together, but his own was not much more than a loose golden bracelet.

'Thread twothri more on it,' Pacey said, 'and then we can git we hats filled and go home to dinner.'

When he looked up again from threading his last two cowslip stalks he saw that Pacey had taken off her brown felt hat. Her uncovered hair was very dark and shining in the sun. At the back it was coiled up into a rich, thick roll, like a heavy sausage. There seemed almost too much hair for her stumpy body and he stared at it amazed.

'Is that all your hair, Pacey?' he said.

'Well, it's what they dished out to me. I ain't had another issue yit.'

'How long is it?' he said. 'It must be very long.'

'Prit near down to me waist.'

'Oh! Pacey,' he said.

As he finished threading his cowslip chain and then joined the ends together he sat staring at Pacey, with her dark hair shining against the blue May sky and her own cowslip chain lying like a gold-green necklace in her lap.

'Does your hair ever come down?' he said, 'or does it always stay up like that?'

'Oh! it comes down a time or two now and again.'

'Let it come down now.'

'It's time to go home to dinner,' Pacey said. 'We got to git back –'

'Please, Pacey,' he said. 'Please.'

'You take your hat and git it filled with cowslips and then we can go –'

'Please,' he said. 'Then I can put my chain on top of your head and it'll look like a crown.'

'Oh! you'd wheedle a whelk out of its shell, you would,' Pacey said. 'You'd wheedle round 'Im up there!'

As she spoke she lifted her face to the blue noon sky so that her spectacles flashed strangely, full of revolving light. A moment later she started to unpin the sausage at the back of her head, putting the black hairpins one by one into her mouth. Then slowly, like an unrolling blind, the massive coil of her hair fell down across her neck and shoulders and back, until it reached her waist.

He had never seen hair so long, or so much of it, and he stared at it with wide eyes as it uncoiled itself, black and shining against the golden cowslip field.

'That's it,' Pacey said, 'have a good stare.'

'Now I've got to put the crown on you,' he said.

He knelt by Pacey's lap and reached up, putting his cowslip chain on the top of her head. All the time he did this Pacey sat very still, staring towards the sun.

'Now yours,' he said.

He reached up, draping Pacey's own longer necklace across her hair and shoulders. The black hair made the cowslips shine more deeply golden than before and the flowers in turn brought out the lights in the hair.

Pacey sat so still and staring as he did all this that he could not tell what she was thinking and suddenly, without asking, he reached up and took off her spectacles.

A strange transformed woman he did not know, with groping blue eyes, a crown on her head and a necklace locking the dark mass of her hair, stared back at him.

'Well, now I suppose you're satisfied?'

'You look very nice, Pacey,' he said. 'You look lovely. I like you.'

'Well, if you're satisfied let's git ready and start back,' Pacey said, 'or else I be blamed if we shan't miss we dinners.'

Hastily, half-blindly, she started to grope with her hands towards her hair.

'And put my specs back on!' she said. 'You took 'em

off. Now put 'em back. How the 'nation do you think I can see 'ithout them?'

'It's not *'ithout*,' he said. 'It's *without*.'

'Oh! *without* then! But put 'em back!'

By the time they began to walk back home his hat was full of cowslips. Pacey's brown felt hat was full too and the basket was brimming over with the flowers that were so like tender, kid-gloved fingers.

At the plank across the stream, as Pacey set down the basket and rested for a moment, he turned and looked back. Once again, as before, the cowslips seemed to stretch without break between himself and the bright noon sky.

'There's just as many as when we came,' he said. 'We didn't make any difference at all, Pacey. You'd think we'd never been, wouldn't you?'

Suddenly, with a cry, Pacey seized him and picked him up, swinging him joyfully round her body and finally holding him upside down.

'Up, round and down!' Pacey said. 'Now what can you see?'

'London!'

Pacey laughed loudly, swinging him a second time and then setting him on his feet again.

When he tried to stand still again he found that the world too was swinging. The cowslip field was rolling like a golden sea in the sun and there was a great trembling about Pacey's hair, her necklace and her little crown of gold.

The Watercress Girl

THE first time he ever went to that house was in the summer, when he was seven, and his grandfather drove him down the valley in a yellow trap and all the beans were in flower, with skylarks singing so high above them in the brilliant light that they hung trembling there like far-off butterflies.

'Who is it we're going to see?' he said.

'Sar' Ann.'

'Which one is Sar' Ann?'

'Now mek out you don' know which one Sar' Ann is,' his grandfather said, and then tickled the flank of the pony with the end of the plaited whip – he always wanted to plait reeds like that himself but he could never make them tight enough – so that the brown rumps, shorn and groomed for summer, quivered like firm round jellies.

'I don't think I've ever seen her,' he said.

'You seen her at Uncle Arth's,' his grandfather said. 'Mek out you don't remember that, and you see her a time or two at Jenny's.' He pronounced it Jinny, but even then the boy could not remember who Jinny was and he knew his grandfather wouldn't tell him until he remembered who Sar' Ann was and perhaps not even after that.

He tried for some moments longer to recall what Sar' Ann was like and remembered presently a square old lady in a pork-pie lace cap and a sort of bib of black jet beads on a large frontal expanse of shining satin. Her eyes were watering. She sat on the threshold of a house that smelled of apples and wax polish. She was in the sun, with a lace-pillow and bone bobbins in a blue and ivory fan on her knees. She was making lace and her hands were covered with big raised veins like the leaves of cabbages when you turned them upside down. He was sure that this was Sar' Ann. He remembered how she had touched his hands with her big cold cabbagy ones and said she would fetch him a cheese-cake, or if he would rather have it a piece of toffee, from the cupboard in her kitchen. She said the toffee was rather sugary and that made him say he preferred the cheese-cake, but his grandfather said:

'Now don't you git up. He's ettin' from morn to night now. His eyes are bigger'n his belly. You jis sit still,' and he felt he would cry because he was so fond of cheese-cake and because he could hardly bear his disappointment.

'She's the one who wanted to give me cheese-cake,' he said, 'isn't she?'

'No, she ain't,' his grandfather said. 'That's your Aunt Turvey.'

'Then is she the one who's married to Uncle Arth? Up the high steps?' he said.

'Uncle Arth ain't married,' his grandfather said. 'That's jis the widder-woman who looks after him.'

His Uncle Arth was always in a night-shirt, with a black scarf round his head. He lived in bed all the time. His eyes were very red. Inside him, so his grandfather said, was a stone and the stone couldn't go up or down but was fixed, his grandfather said, in his kitney, and it was growing all the time.

The stone was an awful nightmare to him, the boy. How big was it? What sort of stone was it? he would say, a stone in the kitney?

'Like a pibble,' his grandfather said. 'Hard as a pibble. And very like as big as a thresh's egg. Very like bigger'n that by now. Very like as big as a magpie's.'

'How did it get there?'

'You're arstin' on me now,' his grandfather said. 'It'd be a puzzle to know. But it got there. And there it is. Stuck in his kitney.'

'Has anybody ever seen it?'

'Nobody.'

'Then if nobody's ever seen it how do they know it's there?'

'Lean forward,' his grandfather said. 'We're gittin' to Long Leys hill. Lean forward, else the shafts'll poke through the sky.'

It was when they climbed slowly up the long wide hill, already white with the dust of early summer, that he became aware of the beans in flower and the skylarks singing so loftily above them. The scent of beans came in soft waves of wonderful sweetness. He saw the flowers on the grey sunlit stalks like swarms of white, dark-throated bees. The hawthorn flower was nearly over and was turning pink wherever it remained. The singing of the skylarks lifted the sky upward, farther and farther, loftier and loftier, and the sun made the blue of it clear and blinding. He felt that all summer was pouring down the hill, between ditches of rising meadowsweet, to meet him. The cold quivering days of coltsfoot flower, the icy-sunny days of racing cloud-shadow over drying ploughland, the dark-white days of April hail, were all behind him, and he was thirsty with summer dust and his face was hot in the sun.

'You ain't recollected her yit, have you?' his grandfather said.

They were at the top of the hill now and below them, in its yellow meadows, he could see the river winding away in broad and shining curves. He knew that that river was at the end of the earth; that the meadows, and with them the big woods of oak and hornbeam and their fading dusty spangles of flower, were another world.

'Take holt o' the reins a minute,' his grandfather said. He put on the brake a notch and the brake shoes scraped on the metal tyres. The boy held the thin smooth reins lightly between his fingers, the way he had been taught to do. He sat forward on the high horse-hair cushions and looked down the long black tramlines of the dead level reins to the brown pony's ears and felt himself, for one moment, high on the hill, to be floating in air, level with all the skylarks above the fields below.

'I'll jis git me bacca going,' his grandfather said. 'We'll be there in about a quartern of hour. You keep holt on her steady.'

He wanted to say to his grandfather that that was a funny word, quartern; his schoolteacher never used that word; and then as he turned he saw the brown, red-veined face softened by the first pulls of tobacco. All the mystery of it was dissolved in a blue sweet cloud. Then his grandfather began coughing because the bacca, he said, had gone down wrong way and was tiddling his gills. His eyes were wet from coughing and he was laughing and saying:

'You know who she is. She's the one with the specs like glarneys.'

Then he knew. She was a little woman, he remembered clearly now, with enormous spy-glass spectacles. They were thick and round like the marbles he played with. She was always whisking about like a clean starched napkin. He had seen her at Uncle Arth's and she had jolted Uncle Arth about the bed with a terrible lack of mercy as she re-made his pillows, smacking them with her lightning hands as if they were disobedient bottoms. The colossal spectacles gave the eyes a terrible look of magnification. They wobbled sometimes like masses of pale floating frog-spawn. He did not like her; he was held in the spawn-like hypnotism of the eyes and dared not speak. She had a voice like a jackdaw's which pecked and mocked at every-body with nasty jabs. He knew that he had got her mixed up somehow and he said:

'I thought the one with the glass eye was Aunt Prunes.'

'Prudence!' his grandfather said. 'They're sisters. She's the young 'un, Prudence.' He spat in a long liquid line, with off-hand care, over the side of the trap. 'Prunes? – that was funny. How'd you come to git holt o' that?'

'I thought everybody else called her Prunes.'

'Oh! You did, simly? Well, it's Prudence. Prudence – that's her proper name.'

Simly was another funny word. He would never under-stand that word. That was another word his schoolteacher never used.

'Is she the one with the moustache?'

'God alive,' the man said. 'Don't you say moustache. You'll git me hung if you say moustache. That's your

20

Aunt Prudence you're talking about. Females don't have moustaches – you know that.'

He knew better than that because Aunt Prunes had a moustache. She was a female and it was quite a long moustache and she had, what was more, a few whiskers on the central part of her chin.

'Why doesn't she shave it off?' he said.

'You watch what you're doing,' his grandfather said. 'You'll have us in the duck-pond.'

'How do you spell it?' he said. 'Her name – Prunes?'

'Here, you gimme holt o' the reins now,' his grandfather said. 'We'll be there in five ticks of a donkey's tail.'

His grandfather took the reins and let the brake off, and in a minute the pony was trotting and they were in a world of high green reeds and grey drooping willows by the river.

'Is it the house near the spinney?' he said.

'That's it,' his grandfather said. 'The little 'un with the big chimney.'

He was glad he remembered the house correctly: not because he had ever seen it but because his grandfather always described it with natural familiarity, as if taking it for granted that he had seen it. He was glad too about Aunt Prunes. It was very hard to get everyone right. There were so many of them, Aunt Prunes and Sar' Ann and Aunt Turvey and Uncle Arth and Jenny and Uncle Ben Newton, who kept a pub, and Uncle Olly, who was a fat man with short black leggings exactly like polished bottles. His grandfather would speak of these people as if they were playmates who had always been in his life and were to be taken for granted naturally and substantially like himself. They were all very old, terribly old, and he never knew, even afterwards, if they were ordinary aunts or uncles or great ones or only cousins some stage removed.

The little house had two rooms downstairs with polished red bricks for floors and white glass vases of dried reeds from the river on the mantelpiece. His grandfather and Aunt Prunes and Sar' Ann and himself had dinner in the room where the stove was, and there were big dishes of potatoes, mashed with thick white butter sauce. Before dinner he sat in the other room with his grandfather and Aunt Prunes and looked at a large leather book called *Sunday at Home*, a prize Aunt Prunes had won at Bible Class, a book in which there were sandwiched, between steel-cuts of men in frock coats and sailors in sailing ships and ladies in black bonnets, pressings of dried flowers thin as tissue from the meadows and the riverside. His contemplation of the flat golden transparencies of buttercup and the starry eyes of bull-daisy and the woolly feathers of grass and reed was ravaged continually by the voice of Sar' Ann, the jackdaw, pecking and jabbing from the kitchen:

'There's something there to keep you quiet. That's a nice book, that is. You can look at that all afternoon.'

'You tell me,' Aunt Prunes said softly, 'when you want another.'

He liked Aunt Prunes. She was quiet and tender. The moustache, far from being forbidding, brushed him with friendly softness, and the little room was so hot with sun and cooking that there were beads of sweat on the whiskers which he made the mistake of thinking, for some time, were drops of the cowslip wine she was drinking. His grandfather had several glasses of cowslip wine and at the third or fourth of them he took off his coat and collar.

At the same time Aunt Prunes bent down and took the book away from him and said:

'You can take off your coat too. That's it. That's better. Do you want to go anywhere?'

'Not yet.'

'When you do it's down the garden and behind the elderberry tree.' Her eyes were a modest brown colour, the same colour as her moustache, and there were many wrinkles about them as she smiled. He could smell the sweetish breath, like the yeast his grandmother used for baking, of the fresh wine on her lips, and she said:

'What would you like to do this afternoon? Tell me what you'd like to do.'

'Read this book.'

'I mean really.'

'I don't know.'

'You do what you like,' she said. 'You go down to the back-brook or in the garden or into the spinney and find snails or sticklebacks or whatever you like.'

She smiled delicately, creating thousands of wrinkles, and then from the kitchen Sar' Ann screeched:

'I'm dishing up in two minutes, you boozers. You'd guzzle there till bulls'-noon if I'd let you.'

Bulls'-noon was another word, another strange queer thing he did not understand.

For dinner they had Yorkshire pudding straight out of the pan and on to the plate, all by itself, as the opening course. Sometimes his grandfather slid slices of the creamy yellow pudding into his mouth on the end of his knife and said he remembered the days when all pudding was eaten first and you had your plate turned upside down, so that you could turn it over when the meat came. Sar' Ann said she remembered that too and she said they were the days and she didn't care what anybody said. People were happier. They didn't have so much of everything but they were happier. He saw Aunt Prunes give a little dry grin whenever Sar' Ann went jabbing on and once he thought he saw her wink at his grandfather. All the time the door of the little room was open so that he could see into the garden with its white pinks and stocks and purple iris flags and now and then he could hear the cuckoo, sometimes near, sometimes far off across the meadows, and many blackbirds singing in endless call and answer in the oak-trees at the end of the garden, where rhubarb and elderberry were in foaming flower together.

'You can hear nightingales too,' Aunt Prunes said. 'Would you like more pudding? You can have more pudding if you want it.'

But his grandfather said again that his eyes were always bigger than his belly and the pudding was put away. 'Ets like a thacker,' his grandfather said and Aunt Prunes said, 'Let him eat then. I like to see boys eat. It does your heart good,' and she smiled and gave him cloudy piles of white potatoes and white sauce from a blue china boat and thin slices of rich beef with blood running out and washing against the shores of his potatoes like the little waves of a delicate pink sea.

'How's Nance and Granny Houghton?' Sar' Ann said, and his grandfather said they were fair-to-mid and suddenly there was great talk of relatives, of grown-ups, of people he did not know, of Charley and a man he thought was named Uncle Fuggles and Cathy and Aunt Em and Maude Rose and two people called Liz and Herbert from Bank Top. His grandfather, who had begun the meal with three or four glasses of cowslip wine and a glass of beer, now helped himself to another glass of beer and then dropped gravy down his waistcoat. Aunt Prunes had beer too and her eyes began to look warm and sleepy and beautifully content.

Afternoon, cuckoo-drowsy, very still and full of sun, seemed to thicken like a web about him long before the meal was over. He thought with dread of the quietness when all of them would be asleep and he himself in the little room with a big boring book and its rustling transparencies of faded flowers. He knew what it was to try to move in the world of grown-up sleep. The whisper of the thinnest page would wake them. Night was the time for sleeping and it was one of the mysteries of life that people could also sleep by day, in chairs, in summertime, in mouth-open attitudes, and with snorting noises and legs suddenly jumping like the legs of horses when the flies were bad.

Then to his joy Aunt Prunes remembered and said:

'You know what I said. You run into the garden and have a look in the spinney for nests. Go down as far as the back-brook if you like.'

'That's it,' his grandfather said. 'You'll very like see a moor-hen's or a coot's or summat down there. Else a pike or summat. Used to be a rare place for pike, a-layin' there a-top o' the water –'

'Don't you git falling in,' Sar' Ann said. 'Don't you git them feet wet. Don't you git them gooseberries – they'll give you belly-ache summat chronic –'

'You bring me some flowers,' Aunt Prunes said. 'Eh? – how's that? You stay a long time, as long as you like, and bring me some flowers.'

There were no nests in the spinney except a pigeon's high up in a hazel-tree that was too thin to climb. He was not quite sure about the song of a nightingale. He knew the blackbird's, full and rich and dark like the bird itself and deep like the summer shadow of the closing wood, and with the voices of thrushes the blackbirds' song filled all the wood with bell-sounds and belling echoes.

Beyond the wood the day was clear and hot. The grass was high to his knees and the ground, falling away, was marshy in places, with mounds of sedge, as it ran down towards the back-brook and the river. He walked with his eyes on the ground, partly because of oozy holes among the sedge, partly because he hoped to see the brown ring of a moor-hen's nest in the marshier places.

It was because of his way of walking that he did not see, for some time, a girl standing up to her knees in red-ochre mud, among half-floating beds of dark-green cresses. But suddenly he lifted his head and saw her standing there, bare-legged and bare-armed, staring at him as if she had been watching him for a long time. Her brown osier cress-basket was like a two-bushel measure and was slung over her shoulder with a strap.

'You don't live here,' she said.

'No,' he said. 'Do you?'

'Over there,' she said. 'In that house.'

'Which house?' He could not see a house.

'You come here and you can see it,' she said.

When he had picked his way through tufts of sedge to where she was standing in the bed of cresses he still could not see a house, either about the wood or across the meadows on the rising ground beyond.

'You can see the chimney smoking,' she said.

'It's not a house. It's a hut,' he said.

'That's where we live.'

'All the time?'

'Yes,' she said. 'You're sinking in.'

The toes of his boots were slowly drowning in red-ochre water.

'If you're coming out here you'd better take your shoes and stockings off,' she said.

A moment or two later his bare feet were cool in the water. She was gathering cresses quickly, cutting them off with an old shoe-knife, leaving young sprigs and trailing skeins of white root behind. She was older than himself, nine or ten, he thought, and her hair hung ribbonless and uncombed, a brown colour, rather like the colour of the basket, down her back.

'Can I gather?' he said, and she said, yes, if he knew what brook-lime was.

'I know brook-lime,' he said. 'Everybody knows brook-lime.'

'Then which is it? Show me which it is. Which is brook-lime?'

That was almost as bad, he thought, as being nagged by Sar' Ann. The idea that he did not know brook-lime from cress seemed to him a terrible insult and a pain. He snatched up a piece in irritation but it did not break and came up instead from the mud-depths in a long rope of dripping red-black slime, spattering his shirt and trousers.

She laughed at this and he laughed too. Her voice, he thought, sounded cracked, as if she were hoarse from shouting or a cold. The sound of it carried a long way. He heard it crack over the meadows and the river with a coarse broken sort of screech that was like the slitting of rag in the deep oppressive afternoon.

He never knew till long afterwards how much he liked that sound. She repeated it several times during the afternoon. In the same cracked voice she laughed at questions he asked or things he did not know. In places the water, shallower, was warm on his feet, and the cresses were a dark polished green in the sun. She laughed because he did not know that anyone could live by gathering cresses. He must be a real town boy, she said. There was only she and her father, she told him, and she began to tell what he afterwards knew were beautiful lies about the way they got up every other day at two in the morning and tramped out to sell cresses in Evensford and Bedford and towns about the valley.

'But the shops aren't open then,' he said and that made her laugh again, cracked and thin, with that long slitting echo across the drowsy meadows.

'It's not in the shops we sell them,' she said. 'It's in the streets – don't you know that? – in the streets –'

And suddenly she lifted her head and drew back her throat and yelled the cry she used in the streets. He had heard that cry before, high and long and melancholy, like a call across lonely winter marshes in its slow fall and dying away, and there was to be a time in his life when it died for ever and he never heard it again:

'Watercree-ee-ee-ee-ee-s! Fresh cre-ee-ee-ee-ee-ee-s! Lovely fresh watercree-ee-ee-ee-ee-ee-s!'

Standing up to his knees in water, his hands full of wet cresses and slimy skeins of roots dripping red mud down his shirt and trousers, he listened to that fascinating sound travelling like a bird-cry, watery and not quite earthly, down through the spinney and the meadows of buttercup and the places where the pike were supposed to lie.

His eyes must have been enormous and transfixed in his head as he listened, because suddenly she broke the note of the cry and laughed at him again and then said:

'You do it. You see if you can do it –'

What came out of his mouth was like a little soprano trill compared with her own full-throated, long-carrying cry. It made her laugh again and she said:

'You ought to come with us. Come with us tomorrow – how long are you staying here?'

'Only today.'

'I don't know where we'll go tomorrow,' she said. 'Evensford, I think. Sometimes we go forty or fifty miles – miles and miles. We go to Buckingham market sometimes – that's forty miles –'

'Evensford,' he said. 'That's where I come from. I could see you there if you go.'

'All right,' she said. 'Where will you be? We come in by The Waggon and Horses – down the hill, that way.'

'I'll be at The Waggon and Horses waiting for you,' he said. 'What time?'

'You be there at five o'clock,' she said. 'Then I'll learn you how to do it, like this – watercree-ee-ee-ee-ee-ee-ee-s! Fresh cree-ee-ee-ee-ee-ee-ee-s! Lovely fresh watercree-ee-ee-ee-ee-ee-s!'

As the sound died away it suddenly seemed to him that he had been there, up to his knees in water, a very long time, perhaps throughout the entire length of the sultry, sun-flushed afternoon. He did not know what time it was. He was cut off from the world of Aunt Prunes and Sar' Ann and his grandfather, the little house and the white pinks and the gooseberry trees, the big boring book whose pages and dead flowers turned over in whispers.

He knew that he ought to go back and said:

'I got to go now. I'll see you tomorrow though – I'll be there. Five o'clock.'

'Yes, you be there,' she said. She wiped a may-fly from her face with her forearm, drawing water and mud across it, and then remembered something. 'You want some cresses for tea? You can take some.'

She plunged her hands into the basket and brought them out filled with cresses. They were cool and wet; and he thought, not only then but long afterwards, that they were the nicest things perhaps anyone had ever given him.

'So long,' she said.

'So long.' That was another funny expression, he thought. He could never understand people who said so long when they seemed to mean, as he did, soon.

She waved her hands, spilling arcs of water-drops in the sun, as he climbed the stile into the spinney and went back. He did his best to wave in answer, but his shoes and stockings were too wet to wear and his hands were full with them and the cresses. Instead he simply stood balanced for a moment on the top bar of the stile, so that she could see him well and then call to him for the last time:

'Cree-ee-ee-ee-ee-es! Lovely fresh cree-ee-ee-ee-ee-es!'

It was only Aunt Prunes who was not angry with him. His grandfather called him 'A young gallus,' and kept saying, 'Where the Hanover've you bin all the time? God A'mighty, you'll git me hung. I'll be burned if I don't git hung,' and Sar' Ann flew about the kitchen with the squawks of a trapped hen, telling him:

'You know what happens to little boys what git wet-foot? And look at your shirt! They git their death, they catch their death. And don't you know who them folks are? Gyppos – that's all they are. Gyppos – they steal things, they live on other folks. That's the sort of folks they are. Don't you go near such folks again – they'll very like keep you and take you away and you'll never see nobody who knows you again. Then we'll find you in the bury-hole.'

But he was not afraid of that and Aunt Prunes only said:

'You didn't bring me my flowers, did you? I like watercress though. I'm glad you brought the watercress. I can have it with my tea.'

It was late before they could start for home again. That was because his socks and shirt took a long time to dry and his shirt had to have an iron run over it several times in case, Sar' Ann kept saying, his mother had a fit. Before getting up into the trap he had to kiss both Sar' Ann and Aunt Prunes, and for some moments he was lost in the horror of the big globular spectacles reflecting and magnifying the evening sun, and then in the friendliness of the dark moustaches below which the warm mouth smiled and said:

'How would you like to stay with me one day? Just you and me in the summer. Would you?'

'Yes,' he said.

'Then you come and see me again, won't you, soon?'

He said Yes, he would see her soon. But in fact he did not see her soon or later or at any time again. He did not go to that house again until he was grown up. That was the day they were burying her and when the cork of silence that passed over the grave had blown out again he felt he could hear nothing but the gassy voice of Sar' Ann, who was old by then but still with the same fierce roving globular eyes, shrilly reminding him of the day he had gathered cresses.

'I'll bet you would never know her now,' she said, 'that girl, would you? Would you ever know that this was her?'

Then she was by his side and he was talking to her: the girl who had gathered the cresses, the same girl who had called with that screeching, melancholy, marshy cry across the summer afternoon. She was not fat but she had a great puffy placidity. She was all in black and her hat had a purple feather in the crown. He remembered the little hut and the brown osier basket on her lithe thin shoulders and he asked her where she lived and what she was doing now. 'In the new houses,' she said. 'I'm Mrs Corbett now.' She took him to the garden hedge and pointed out to him blocks of bricks, like the toys of gigantic children, red and raw and concrete fenced, lining the road above the valley.

That was the road where he and his grandfather had driven down on that distant summer morning, when the beans were in flower and he had got so mixed with his relatives and had wondered how Aunt Prunes had spelled her name.

'That's us,' she said. She pointed with stout and podgy finger, a trifle nervously but with pride, across the fields. 'The second one. The one with the television. Have you got television?'

'No.'

'You ought to have it,' she said. 'It's wonderful to see things so far away. Don't you think it's wonderful?'

'Wonderful,' he said.

But on the night he drove home as a boy, watching the sky of high summer turn from blue to palest violet and then more richly to purple bronze and the final green-gold smokiness of twilight, he did not know these things. He sat still on the cushions of the trap, staring ahead. The evening was full of the scent of bean flowers and he was searching for early stars.

'Shall we light the lamps?' he said.

And presently they lit the lamps. They too were golden. They seemed to burn with wonderful brightness, lighting the grasses of the roadside and the flowers of the ditches and the crowns of fading may. And though he did not know it then they too were fading, for all their brightness. They too were dying, along with the things he had done and seen and loved: the little house, the cuckoo day, the tender female moustaches and the voice of the watercress girl.

Let's Play Soldiers

THE yellow strings of laburnum flower had already faded that afternoon when I stood on sentry for the 1st Battalion Albion Street Light Infantry and Mrs Strickland came out of her kitchen door wearing a sack apron and a man's check cap pinned on her spindly curling rags by a long black hat pin and started shaking mats against the garden fence, not three yards from the tent made of split sacks and old lace curtains where we of the battalion held councils of war before going into battle.

Upstairs across the yard Mrs Rankin was sitting at a window with a bottom like a pumpkin hanging over the sill, huffing energetically on glass already as pure as crystal and then scrupulously polishing the vapour off again with a spotless yellow rag.

The face of Mrs Rankin, smooth and clean as porcelain, looked as if it had been polished too but the face of Mrs Strickland, like her curl-ragged hair, had nothing but greyness in it, a dopey salty greyness at the same time hard, so that the skin looked like scoured pumice stone.

I was only six at the time and still a private; but I thought I detected a smell of parsnip wine in the air. Mangled dust and shreds of coco-matting rose in dense brown clouds as Mrs Strickland beat the decaying mats against the fence but I stood unshakably at attention under the laburnum tree, head up, eyes straight ahead, right hand firmly on the umbrella we were using as a rifle because Jeddah Clarke, our Captain, had the air gun, the only other weapon we possessed.

I knew that if I stood firm on guard and didn't flinch and saluted properly and challenged people and didn't let them pass until they gave the password, I might become, in time, a lance-corporal. There was nothing on earth I wanted more than to be a lance-corporal: except perhaps to kill a soldier.

'I wisht Albie was here,' Mrs Strickland said. 'I wisht Albie was here.'

It wasn't only that morning that her voice had that pumice-dry melancholy in it. It was always there, like the curling rags. Sometimes Mrs Strickland didn't take out the curling rags until after Bill Strickland came home for his bloater tea at six o'clock and sometimes she didn't take them out at all.

'Ain't got a spare Daisy, gal, I reckon?'

Mrs Strickland, staring with diffused and pleading eyes through the dust she had raised, groping up towards the sumptuous pumpkin of Mrs Rankin on the window sill, ran a dreary hand several times across her brow.

'Ain't got nivry one left,' Mrs Rankin said. 'You had the last one yisty.'

Daisies were a brand of headache powder guaranteed to refresh and free you from pain in five minutes. Mrs Strickland was taking them all day.

'Ain't Bill a-workin' then?'

'Bad a-bed. Can't lift 'isself orf the piller. I wisht Albie was here.'

I knew Albie couldn't be there. Albie, who was eighteen, a private too like me, was in France, fighting the Germans. I liked Albie; he had a ginger moustache and was my friend. Every other day or so I asked Mrs Strickland if and when Albie was going to become a lance-corporal, but somehow she never seemed to think he was.

'Ain't you got nivry one tucked away, gal, some-wheer?'

'Nivry one,' Mrs Rankin said. 'Nivry one.'

Despair wrapped Mrs Strickland's face in a greyer, dustier web of gloom.

'Me 'ead's splittin'. It'll split open. I wisht Albie was here.'

'Won't the boy nip and get y' couple? Ask the boy.'

Mrs Strickland, seeming to become aware of me for the first time, turned to my impassive sentinel figure with eyes of greyest supplication.

'Nip down the shop and fetch us a coupla Daisies, there's a good boy. Nip and ask your mother to lend us a thrippenny bit, there's a good boy. I left me puss up-stairs.'

It was funny, my mother always said, how Mrs Strickland was always leaving, losing or mislaying her purse somewhere.

'And a penn'orth o' barm too, boy, while you're down there. I gotta make a mite o' bread, somehow,' she called up to Mrs Rankin. 'Ain't got a mite in the place, gal. Not so much as a mossel.'

Mrs Rankin, who would presently be hurrying down to the yard to scour and white-wash the kitchen steps to blinding glacier whiteness and who, as my mother said, almost polished the coal before putting it on the fire, merely turned on Mrs Strickland a rounder, blanker, completely unhelpful pumpkin.

I didn't move either; I was on guard and Jeddah Clarke said you could be shot if you moved on guard.

'Nip and ask your mother to lend us a thrippenny bit, boy. Tanner if she's got it, boy –'

'I can't go, Mrs Strickland. I'm on sentry,' I said. 'I'll get shot.'

'Kids everywhere,' Mrs Strickland said, 'and nivry one on 'em to run of arrant for you when you want. I wisht Albie was here.'

Mrs Strickland dragged the decaying mats to the middle of the yard. The smell of parsnip wine went with her and she called up to Mrs Rankin:

'Ain't got 'arf a loaf I can have for a goin' on with, gal, I reckon? Jist till the baker gits here? Jist 'arf? Jist the top?'

'You want one as'll fit on the bottom I lent you the day afore yisty? or will a fresh 'un do?'

Fiery, tempestuous white curls seemed to fly suddenly out of Mrs Strickland's mournful, aching head.

'What's a matter wi' y'? Askt y' a civil question, dint I? Askt y' civil question. What's a matter wi' y' all of a pop?'

'Sick on it,' Mrs Rankin said. 'About sick to death on it.'

'Go on, start maungin'! Start yelpin'!'

'Yelpin', yelpin'? Ain't got nothing to yelp about, I reckon, have I? When it ain't bread it's salt. When it ain't salt it's bakin' powder. Enough to gie y' the pip. When it ain't –'

'Keep on, keep on!' Mrs Strickland said. 'It'll do your fat gullet good. And me with 'im in bed. And the damn war on. And Albie not here.'

Suddenly she dropped the mats, picked up a bucket from the kitchen drain and started beating and rattling it like a war-gong. In a flash Mrs Rankin's pumpkin darted through the window, dragging the sash down behind it. Behind the crystal glass Mrs Rankin's face remained palely distorted, mouthing furiously.

Down below in the yard, Mrs Strickland rattled the bucket again, shaking her curling rags, and yelled:

'Mag, mag. Jaw, jaw. That's all folks like you are fit for. Mag, jaw, mag, jaw –'

Mrs Rankin's face, ordinarily so polished and composed, splintered into uncontrollable furies behind the glass as Mrs Strickland started to fill the bucket with water from the stand-pipe in the yard.

In a second Mrs Rankin had the window up with a shrilling squeak of the sash and was half leaping out:

'And don't you start your hanky-pankies. Don't you start that! – I oiled and polished my door! –'

An arc of white water struck Mrs Rankin's back door like a breaker. Mrs Rankin slammed down the window and started beating the panes with her fists. Mrs Strickland screamed that she wisht Albie was here, Albie would let some daylight into somebody, and threw the bucket with a crashing roll across the yard.

A moment later a bedroom window shot open in the Strickland house and an unsober chin of black stubble leaned out and bawled:

'What the bloody 'ell's going on down there? If you

two don't shut your yawpin' chops I'll come down and lay a belt acrosst the pair on y' –'

'I wisht Albie was here!' Mrs Strickland said. 'I wisht Albie was here!'

Drearily she slammed away into the house and after that it was silent for some minutes until suddenly from the street beyond the yard I could hear the inspiring note of war cries. A minute later the first battalion Albion Street Light Infantry came triumphantly pounding down the path between the cabbage patches, led by Jeddah Clarke, carrying the air-gun, Wag Chettle, bearing the standard, a red handkerchief tied to a bean-pole, and Fred Baker, beating a drum he had had for Christmas.

Fred and Jeddah were actually in khaki uniforms. Jeddah, besides the air-gun, wore a bandolier across his chest with real pouches and two clips of spent cartridges; Fred had a peaked khaki cap on, with the badge of the Beds & Bucks Light Infantry on one side and that of the Royal Welch Fusiliers on the other. At that time the Fusiliers were billeted in the town and we had an inspired admiration for them because they kept a white goat as mascot. The goat ate anything you gave it, even cigarettes.

What now surprised me about the battalion was not its air of triumph but its size. Usually it was no more than eight strong. Now it was twenty. Those bringing up the rear were even flying a second flag. It was a square of blue-and-white football shirt. I caught the gleam of a second and even a third air-gun and then suddenly Jeddah Clarke, our Captain, raised his air-gun and yelled:

'Gas Street are on our side! They're in the battalion! Gas Street have come in with us! Charge!'

We all cheered madly and charged. The little hairs of my neck stuck up in pride, excitement and admiration as we thundered dustily into the summer street outside.

'Charge!' we all shouted. 'Charge! Capture 'em! Charge!'

Heady with thought of battle, we wheeled like thunder into Winchester Street: completely unnoticed by a milk float, two bakers' carts, a chimney sweep on a bicycle and two women pushing prams.

'Charge!' I yelled, and was stunned to hear the blast of a bugle, suddenly blown at my side by a boy named Charley Fletcher, who was in the Lads' Brigade.

This new note, defiant above the roll of Fred Baker's drum, had us all in a frenzy of battle just as we surged past a railway dray loading piles of bulky leather outside a factory, where the crane swung out from its fourth storey door like a gallows and dropped its thirty feet of rippling chain down to the shining hot pavement below.

'Charge!' I yelled, bringing up the rear with the umbrella under my arm and pointing it forward as if it had a bayonet in the end, exactly as I had seen in pictures of soldiers charging from the trenches. There was nothing we didn't know about soldiers and the trenches. We knew all about Vimy Ridge, Ypres, Hill 60 and Verdun too. We had seen them all in pictures.

The voice of our Captain, Jeddah Clarke, tore the air with fresh challenge as we whipped out of Winchester Street into Green's Alley. Continually Charley Fletcher's bugle ripped the quiet of the afternoon to shreds with raucous notes that were almost hysterical, rallying both us and the reinforcements of Gas Street, and I wondered suddenly where we were going and where the attack would be made.

Jeddah, yelling, told us all a moment later:

'Down to The Pit! We'll git 'em in The Pit!'

My heart went absolutely icy, turned sour and dropped to my stomach.

The Pit was a terrible place. You never went to The Pit. No one ever did. If you did you never came out alive. The people there, who lived in sordid back-to-back hovels with sacks at the windows, captured you, tied you up, locked you in satanic privies and let you suffocate to death. If they didn't do that they starved you, took away all your clothes and sold you naked in slavery. They were the most awful people in the world. People like Mrs Strickland were respectable by comparison. They were always dirty, drunk and fighting. They were always stinking and they were full of bugs and fleas.

I suddenly wanted to turn back, stand guard in the cabbage patch and dream quietly about being a lance-corporal one day.

'Charge!' everyone yelled. 'Charge! Git the stones ready!'

Out of Green's Alley we swung on the tide of battle into The Jetty, a narrow track of dried mud and stone. There the triumphant column broke up for a moment or two and we began to hack stones from the dust with the heels of our boots. By this time my legs and knees were shaking: so much so that all I could hack out were two pebbles and the stopper of a broken beer bottle. But Fred Baker, seeing this, took pity on me and armed me with half a brick.

The bugle sounded again, shrill as a cornet.

'Air-guns in front!' Jeddah yelled. 'Git ready when I say charge!'

We thundered on. We had been joined now by a butcher's boy on a bicycle and for some reason I found myself clinging to his saddle. Suddenly in the excitement the butcher's boy started pedalling madly and I could hardly keep up with the column as it pounded along.

Less than a minute later we were facing the jaws of The Pit. They were nothing more than a gap between two rows of derelict gas-tarred fences but beyond them I could see the little one-storey hovels with sacks at their windows, the horrible squat brick prisons of outdoor privies and a few dirty flags of shirt on a washing line.

It was impossible for my heart to turn cold a second time; it was frozen stiff already. But the paralysis that kept it stuck at the pit of my stomach now affected my legs and I stopped running.

This, as it turned out, was a purely instinctive reaction. Everyone else had stopped running too.

'Charge!' someone yelled and this time it was not our Captain, Jeddah.

The order came from behind us and as we turned in its direction we found ourselves the victims of the oldest of all battle manoeuvres. We were being attacked in the rear.

This time my eyes froze. The Pit Brigade stood waiting for us: eight or ten of them, headed by a black-mouthed deaf-mute armed with five-foot two-pronged hoe. Another had an ugly strip of barrel hoop sharpened up like a sword and another a catapult with a black leather sling big enough to hold an egg. He was smoking a cigarette. Two others were manning a two-seater pram armoured with rusty plates of corrugated iron and this, we all realized, was an armament we did not possess. It was the first tank we had encountered.

The deaf-mute started showing his black teeth, gurgling strange cries. He made vigorous deaf-and-dumb signs with his hands and the snarling faces about him jabbered. The entire Pit Brigade, older, bigger, dirtier and better armed than we were, stood ready to attack.

It was too late to think about being a lance-corporal now and a moment later they were on us.

'Charge!' everyone shouted from both sides. 'Charge!' and we were an instant clash of bricks, stones, catapults, flags, sticks and air-guns that would not fire. Above it all the unearthly voice of the deaf mute gurgled like a throttled man, mouthing black nothings.

I threw my brick. It fell like the legendary sparrow through the air. Someone started to tear the coat off my back and I thrashed madly about me with the umbrella. I could see our two flags rocking ship-mast fashion in the centre of battle and Charley Fletcher using the bugle as a hammer. The two-pronged hoe fell like a claw among us and the armour plates fell off the pram-tank as it ran into Fred Baker and cut his legs, drawing first blood.

Soon we actually had them retreating.

'We're the English!' I heard Jeddah shouting. 'We're the English! The Pit are the bloody Germans,' and this stirring cry of patriotism roused us to fresh thrills of battle frenzy.

'We're the English!' we all yelled. 'We're the English!'

Suddenly as if a trap door had opened the Pit Brigade, under sheer weight of pressure, fell backward into the jaws of The Pit, hastily slamming the door behind them as a barricade and leaving outside a single stray soldier armed with a rusty flat-iron suspended on a piece of cord and dressed as a sergeant of the Royal Artillery, complete with spurs and puttees.

Cut off from the tide of battle, this soldier gave several rapid and despairing looks about him, dropped the flat-iron and bolted like a hare.

'Prisoner!' Jeddah yelled. 'Prisoner! Git him! Take him prisoner!'

In a moment Fred Baker, Charley Fletcher and myself were after him. We caught him at the top of The Jetty. At first he lay on his back and kicked out at us with the spurs, spitting at the same time, but soon I was sitting on his face, Fred Baker on his chest and Charley Fletcher, who was the eldest, on his legs. For a long time he kept trying to spit at us and all the time there was a strong, putrid, stinking, funny smell about him.

We kept him prisoner all afternoon. Then we decided to strip him. While Fred and I sat on his face and chest Charley unrolled the puttees and took off the spurs.

'You always have spoils of war when you take prisoners,' Charley explained. 'Soldiers call it a bit of buckshee.'

We spent some time arguing about how the buckshee should be divided and finally Charley was awarded the puttees, because he was the eldest, and Fred Baker and I each had a spur. Having the spur was even better than being a lance-corporal and I couldn't remember ever having had anything that made me feel more proud.

It was almost evening before Jeddah and the rest of the Battalion got back, fifty strong, from telling of our victory in far places, in Lancaster Street, Rectory Street, Bedford Row, King's Lane and those parts of the town who could not be expected to hear of our triumph other than by word of mouth and from us.

'We still got the prisoner, Captain,' we said. 'What shall we do with him?'

'Shoot him,' Jeddah said.

Orders were orders with Jeddah and we asked if we could have the air-gun.

He handed it over.

'I leave it to you,' Jeddah said. He was now wearing a forage cap, three long service stripes, a leather belt and a Welch black flash he had captured. 'Charge!'

The sound of returning triumph from the fifty-strong battalion had hardly died away before we set to work to shoot the flat-iron boy.

First of all we made him stand up by the fence, among a pile of junk and nettles. By this time we had tied his hands and legs with the cord off the flat-iron and had taken off his shoes so that he found it hard to run. But he still spat at us as he stood waiting to be shot and he still had that funny, sickening smell.

Fred Baker shot him first. The unloaded air-gun made a noise rather like a damp squib. Then Charley Fletcher shot him and the gun made a noise like a damp squib a second time. Then I shot him and as I did so I made a loud, realistic noise that was more like the crack of a bursting paper bag. I aimed between the eyes of the flat-iron boy as I shot and I was very thrilled.

'Now you're dead,' we said to him. 'Don't you forget. Don't you move – you're dead. You can't fight no more.'

He didn't look very dead when we left him but we knew he was. We told the Captain so when we rejoined the battalion in Gas Street, Fred Baker blowing the bugle and wearing the artillery puttees, Charley Fletcher and I taking turns to carry the air-gun and both of us waving a spur.

Jeddah was drunk with victory. 'Tomorrow we're goin' to charge The Rock!' he said. The Rock was even worse than The Pit but now none of us was appalled and all of us cheered. There was no holding us now.

'We'll kill 'em all!' Jeddah said. 'We'll burn ole Wag Saunders at the stake.' Wag was their Captain. 'Just like Indians. We'll win 'em. We ain't frit. Who are we?'

'We're the English!' we yelled.

It was already growing dark when I trotted home through the streets with my spur. In the back yard there were no lights in Mrs Rankin's neat, white-silled windows and in Mrs Strickland's house all the blinds were drawn although all the lights were on.

'Where have you been all this long time?' my father said.

He sat alone in the kitchen, facing a cold rice pudding. My father was very fond of cold rice pudding but tonight he did not seem to want it. Under the green gaslight the brown nutmeg skin of it shone unbroken.

'Fighting with our battalion,' I said.

I told him how the battle had been won and how I had captured the spur.

'That spur doesn't belong to you,' he said. 'Tomorrow morning you must take it back.'

I felt sick with disappointment and at the way grown-up people didn't understand you.

'Can I keep it just for tonight?'

'Just for tonight,' he said. 'But you must take it back tomorrow.'

Then I remembered something and I told him how the boy I'd got it from was dead.

'How is that?' he said. 'Dead?'

'We shot him.'

'Oh! I see,' he said. 'Well: tomorrow you go and find the dead boy and give him back his spur.'

Looking round the kitchen I now remembered my mother and asked where she was.

'She's with Mrs Strickland,' my father said. 'Mrs Rankin's with her too. I expect you noticed that all the blinds were drawn?'

I said I had noticed and did it mean that someone was dead?

'It's your friend – your friend Albie's not going to come back,' my father said.

After that my father didn't seem to want to speak very much and I said:

'Could I go and play in the tent until mother comes home?'

'You can go and play in the tent,' he said.

'With a candle?' I said. 'It's dark now outside.'

'Take a candle if you like,' he said.

I took a candle and sat in the tent all by myself, looking
at my spur. It was shaped something like a handcuff to
which was attached a silver star. The candlelight shone
down on the spur with wonderful brilliance and as I
looked at it I remembered the voices of Mrs Strickland
and Mrs Rankin squabbling with bitterness over a loaf of
bread in the afternoon and how Mrs Strickland wisht that
Albie would come back, and now I listened again for
their voices coming from the outer darkness but all I
could hear was the voice from the afternoon:

'I wisht Albie was here. I wisht Albie was here.'

There is nothing much you can do with a solitary
candle and a single spur. The spur can only shine like
silver and the candlelight with a black vein in the heart
of it.

Early next morning I took the spur back to The Pit.
I ran all the way there and I was glad that no one saw
me. The sun was coming up over the gas-tarred fences,
the little hovels, the privies and the washing lines and all
I did was to lay the spur on a stone in the sunlight,
hoping that someone would come and find it there.

I ran all the way home, too, as hard as I could: afraid
of the enemy we had conquered and the soldier I had
killed.

The Far Distant Journey

HE was only six when his father took him on that first far distant journey, through strange countryside, into another county, to a place he did not know. It was the time of year when all the colours of the fields seemed to be one colour, seen through a grey cloth of sooty rain, and the engines of the three separate trains in which he travelled were sulky-bellied monsters, gasping forward in the half-fog of smelly, steamy air.

After the third train his father and himself were in a big, high station. Above him was a double-winged glass roof that hung there like the wings of a giant crow. The engines of trains standing in the station made hoarse gyrating breathless sounds. The trains bore on the sides of them long names wreathed in steam that smelled of cooking. He was aware of the faces of passengers seen through holes of steamy glass, like broken ice, as they peered out with bored hope across platforms. A great mass of smoke rose against the crow's wings. All was black. His father was black too: black overcoat, black hard hat, black shoes, black-pointed waxed moustache and black umbrella. Only his gloves were brown and his eyes a bright soft blue as they stared at the world of echoing smoky monsters.

Then his father and himself were in another place, in another part of the station. It had a long curved marble counter. On it there were copper geysers with rows of gas-blue grinning teeth. At many round marble tables with ferns on them and pots of yellow mustard many people sat eating and drinking. Frightening steam flew from geyser taps at unexpected moments, making him jump, reminding him of the barber's shop where his father went to be shaved.

His father was incredibly at home in this place. He took off his coat and hat and gloves and hung them up on a hat-stand with his umbrella.

'Would you like a big poached egg on toast? Or would you rather have a sandwich?'

'A samwidge.'

'And a nice hot cup of cocoa?'

'Yes.'

'Yes what? I don't hear anything.'

'Please.'

'That's the ticket.'

A lady with starched cap and large white butterfly apron-strings was standing over the table where his father and himself were sitting.

'Would the sandwiches be ham?'

'Ham, sir. Yes.'

'Very well. One ham sandwich. Two poached eggs on toast. And two cups of cocoa.'

When the sandwich arrived the lady also put before him, beside his plate, a little pot of mustard. She even opened it; and his father, when she had gone, smiled for the first time that day.

'She thinks you're a man. She thinks you like mustard.'

'Yes.'

'But you don't, do you?'

'No.' His father was watching him. 'No thank you.'

'That's the ticket. Eat your sandwich while it's hot. We've got a good way to go.'

He knew, of course, that he ought to have laughed at his father's remark about the sandwich being hot. But the sandwich was not only cold. It was also very big. He could scarcely hold it with both hands. It was cut triangularwise and pieces of fat fell out of it. Then he felt the bread sticking in his throat. He could not swallow and he found himself looking up at his father's face, seeing on it once again the dreadfully strange remote expression he had seen so often in the trains.

'Can't you get through it all?'

'I don't like the fat.'

'Never mind,' his father said. 'I'll wrap it in my clean handkerchief. You'll be glad of it later. Have you got a handkerchief?'

'Yes.'

'Blow then. Blow hard.'

After that they were in a street of trams. The trams were like drunken ships, reeling down canals of black water. Big bells donged in the foggy rain. A great bridge, scalded black at the edges, went over a street and it was dark under the bridge except for the blue sparks of tram-wires and the fiery ovens of chestnut sellers sheltering from the rain.

Then they were walking. There were no trams. The causeways of the street were high up, with steps and railings. It was an old place. Black entries were cut between the houses. There were many holes in the pavements where the rain was black.

His father stopped on the high causeway and closed his umbrella.

'This is where we're going,' he said. 'Remember to take your cap off.'

After that they were in a little shop. Just over the threshold there was a piece of sack on the floor. 'Wipe your feet,' his father said and he began to say 'It's not a proper door-mat. It's only a sack,' but his father made terrible, hissing train-like noises of remonstrance and a bell on a spring jangled far-away down a passage, echoing emptily.

It was a long time before anyone answered that bell. He became aware, as he waited, of strange creatures staring down at him from glass cases on the walls. A fox was one of them. It was an old, shabby, yellow fox and was running among yellow grasses. There was a stoat too, almost a white stoat, with glass eyes like pink shoe buttons, and a heron, grey like the winter day.

Then she was in the shop. He did not know at all how she had suddenly managed to get there. She was grey like the heron and old and shabby like the fox. She was tall, with shining yellow hands and throat and a long black skirt that came down below her ankles. She was so old and far off and fearsome in her deathly tallness that he was terrified when she came down to him, kneeling, touching with her skinniness his own small hands.

'Is this the boy?'

Perhaps I am going to stay with her, he thought. Perhaps she is going to keep me.

'Yes. Say how do you do to Aunt.'

'How do you do.'

She fixed on him eyes that were globular and bloodless with a queer fondness.

'Not hard to see who he features,' she said.

After that they were sitting, the three of them, in a little room behind the shop. It was not like home. Until that moment there had been excluded from his experience any idea that there might be rooms in the world that were not like home. The table in the centre of the room had no cloth on it. There was no carpet and no mat on the floor. A black horse-hair chair from which the stuffing was coming out like old frizzly whiskers stood on one side of the fireplace and his father sat in it, holding his bowler hat on his knees.

'I bin thinking about you,' she said. 'It was about your time to come.'

'That's right.'

'How old is the boy now?'

'Six.'

That was always the time, he thought, when old people like her groped into cupboards and came to you with peppermints or cake or biscuits or oranges to keep you quiet while they spoke of other things.

But it did not happen this time. He thought it strange that she had nothing to give. She was the first old lady he had ever known who had nothing to give.

'Have you seen Joe?' she said.

'Not yet,' his father said. 'We came straight up.'

'You'll see him before you go, won't you?' she said. 'He's down at Market. He'd like to see you, Joe would.'

Then his father and the old woman began to talk, gradually forgetful of him, in growing darkness. The rain on the backyard outside was figured with smoky, lowering mists. The walls of the room stared out, like those of the shop, with the wild dead eyes of creatures imprisoned in cases. He felt imprisoned too. Darkness began chaining and confusing him and filling him with fears.

'It's time to light the gas. Can we light the gas?' he said.

His father let out once again the awful hissing train-like noises of remonstration.

'Sit still! Sit still,' his father said. 'Don't be a whittle-breeches.'

'I can find a light,' she said. 'Somewhere.'

Then he was made aware of another unbelievable, mystifying, terrible thing. There was no gas in that house. A candle borne before her face threw into upward elongations the drawn fissures of her long neck. The flame waved flatly above its enamel holder as she set it down on the table. Then he knew how much he hated candlelight. He hated all its shadowy wanderings. He wanted the singing, greenish, friendly glow of gas, the first beautiful plop of the red-flared mantle destroying dark with whiteness.

He felt a great lump swell in his throat. A house without gas, without a cloth on the table, without even a bit-hearthrug on the floor: that must be a terribly poor house, he thought, the poorest he had ever known, and he sat there imprisoned and haunted by its candle-shadows until the lump of homesickness and fear was too big in his throat to swallow.

'Have you been up there?' she asked.

'No. Not today.'

'Are you going up there?'

'Not with the boy,' he said. 'It's too far with the boy.'

'I hoped it'd be a better day than this for you,' she said. 'We had a lot of days a good deal like this when she was here.'

His father did not speak.

'That was one of them slopping, dirty winters. Up to your neck. I recollect how the water used to run like rivers off the causeways.'

His father did not speak. His face, old as it then seemed to the boy, as he afterwards knew, only a young face, was white and disturbed and set hard beyond the candle-flame.

'It was a day like this when they took her up there,' she said. 'Only colder than this. Not fit to turn a dog out. Nor a cat, nor nobody.'

His father still had nothing to say.

'You ever hear from him?' she said.

'Christmas.' His father spoke now with a checked, far-off voice. 'Every Christmas time.'

'I'd Christmas the skin off his back,' she said, 'if I could.'

'Little pigs,' his father said. 'Little pigs.'

'Well, and what are their ears for?' she said. 'They've got to hear sometime, haven't they?'

'What they don't hear,' his father said, 'they don't grieve over.'

'Grieve,' she said, 'grieve, my dear God, grieve – you may well talk about grieve.'

'I know, I know,' he said. 'But that's all done with now.'

'She was like a tallow candle,' the old lady said. 'No more to her 'n a tallow candle. And not much of it at that.'

That was the moment when his hatred of candlelight went deeper still. He felt he could not bear the awful, melancholy wandering light of it. He could not bear the hollow carvings of the shrunken face made so old and fearsome by the light and the shadows. He wondered for several minutes if she would cry – but to his everlasting surprise she did not cry. In her face there was only a stony, thin-jowled hatred of something that frightened him then and that he long remembered.

He saw his father stir at last in the chair. He felt the lump in his throat ready to burst with rapture as he took his large silver watch from his pocket.

'Well, we ought to be getting on.'

Then his father got up and took from his inside pocket an envelope which he laid on the table.

'Oh! no, no, no, no,' she said.

'You take it,' his father said. 'Take it.'

She did not speak this time but she took his hands fiercely in hers and clenched them. Even then she did not cry. Her face was terribly fleshless and dry in the candlelight and the boy reached, at that moment, a strange and long-enduring conclusion about the old.

There must be a time, he thought, when they were so old and dry that their tears could not flow any more. That could only be it. And no doubt there would come a time, he thought, when he, too, like her, would be able to cry for things no longer.

'What did you give her?' he said to his father, out on the high causeway.

'Just a little something.'

'Some money?'

'Just a little something.'

The streets were blue with twilight and trams were dancing past chestnut ovens, flashing their sparking fires.

'Are we going to see Joe now?'

'We won't have time to see Joe,' his father said. 'We want some tea before we catch the train.'

'Who is Joe?'

'He's your uncle. My uncle.'

'Is he married to that lady?'

'Yes.'

'And who was she?' he said. 'The one you were talking about? The one who was like the tallow candle?'

'Her sister.'

That was all his father answered. Later the three trains roared him home, under friendly gas-light, through the rainy night-time. And then there was no more speaking of the old lady, the house with the candle and the woman who was like a candle until, in the last train, they were nearly home.

'Did you understand what we were talking about back there?' his father said.

'No.'

'That's just as well. There's no need,' his father said.

How could someone be like a tallow candle? he thought. He was troubled by that as he had been troubled by the shadows of the candle in that dark and gas-less room. Was it because she was pale and alone and dying,

perhaps in that house, that they spoke of her like that?
Because in time the flame of her died and went out? – he
could only think that that was it.

'What was her name?' he said.

His father began to feel in his pocket for something.

'Could you eat the rest of the sandwich? I saved it for
you.'

'Yes please.'

'That's the ticket,' his father said. 'That was funny,
wasn't it, when the waitress thought you liked mustard?'

'Yes.'

He held the sandwich in both hands and stared at it.
He did not want it very much.

'Did she die?' he said.

But his father did not speak or look at him. It was
exactly as if he himself had not spoken, and there was no
answer except the shriek of the train carrying him home,
after his first far distant journey, through the sleepy
night-time.

The Pemberton Thrush

IT was not his father who first called her The Pemberton Thrush. That was a name invented by the music critic on a north of England newspaper in her native town. Afterwards she came southward. She was a small, dark-haired girl with soft white skin and friendly, brimming eyes.

He was not quite seven when he first heard her sing. They were the days when his father had organised a quartette for mixed voices and when the little front parlour of the house, with its fretted walnut piano and three Dresden vases on the slate mantelpiece and pots of asparagus fern on the bay window-sills, was so often full of the sound of singing. In those days his father was passionately fond of unaccompanied part songs.

One of three Dresden vases, the largest one, the one that always stood in the centre, had a dancing scene, mostly in rose and green, painted on the front of it. Several girls, all rather plump and with flowing skirts and hair, were depicted dancing in a garden, between lacy trees and in front of terraces and statuary. He could not help thinking that the Pemberton Thrush, or Miss Mortenson as he first knew her and as she really was, looked so like the principal figure on that vase. She had the same fresh, soft-skinned, charming grace, the same way of holding the tips of the fingers of her hands just touching each other, as if neither of them could bear to part.

It was on a cold December evening that he first heard

her sing. After he had put his red felt slippers on and his nightgown he was sometimes allowed to come down for a few minutes to eat his basin of bread and milk, or his mutton broth with bread in it, in the kitchen. He liked the mutton broth best; the bread swam in it better; his ships didn't sink so soon. It also kept hot longer, so that he couldn't eat it so fast and had to stay up later, blowing it hard, and there were many wonderful little blobs of golden fat in it that reflected the gas-light like hundreds of little moons.

That night the broth was hotter than usual. The tip of the spoon kept burning his tongue no matter how much he blew and made storms so that his ships rocked against the shores of the basin. He played a lot with the ships, until at last his mother said he was dainty.

'Eat it up,' she said. 'I don't like little boys who are dainty.'

He kept saying the broth was too hot, but what he was really doing most of the time was to listen to the sound of singing from the front parlour and wish that he were there, where the fire had been specially lighted and candles were burning on the curly brass arms of the piano.

'Can I go and say good-night to father while it gets cold?'

'All right. Quickly though. Look sharp and come back. They don't want to be bothered with you in there.'

Then he was in the front room. It was as he always liked to picture it: the fire burning with blue leaves of flame because it was so cold outside, the candles shining on the nutty golden veneer of the piano, the pages of sheet music lying about the sofa and the chairs.

'I came to say good-night.'

'Very well, then. Say good-night to everybody. And look slippy.'

It was nice when his father said things like 'look slippy'; then he knew that there was really no chance of his being sharp or angry.

First he said good-night to Miss Flavell. She was the soprano. She had a rather long neck which was enclosed in a sort of lace stocking that was kept stiff with pieces of bone in the sides. She was quite tall and her hair had a touch of pale ginger. The same touch of ginger was responsible for the fact that sometimes he thought her eyes hadn't any lashes.

'Good-night, Miss Flavell.'

He was never really at ease with Miss Flavell, who bent rather stiffly. Then Mr Welsh, the tenor, a very dapper man with moustaches screwed and waxed to excruciating comical points, actually shook hands with him and pretended he was a man and called him Mister B. He always did that. Everything about him smelled of violet brilliantine.

'Well, good-night, Mister B. Sleep well and don't fall out of bed, Mister B.'

That was because he had once had a nightmare and had fallen out of bed with a loud bump while the quartette were still singing. Mr Welsh had never forgotten it and thought it was very funny.

'Now you don't know this lady, do you?'

'No.'

'This is Miss Mortenson. She comes from a long way away.'

'Where?'

'Up in the north. A long, long way away. She's come to live here.'

Then she was stooping to say good-night to him. Unlike Miss Flavell she did not merely bend. She actually stooped, almost on her knees, so that her face was level and close to him.

'Not shy, are you?'

'No.'

Her eyes were wonderfully warm and dark. Her skin was very soft when she touched his hands. He felt he could never be shy with such friendly brimming eyes, so warm under their masses of dark brown hair.

'How old are you?'

'Six and in my seven.'

'Seven? That's lucky, isn't it? That's a lucky number.'

She had a little blue enamel watch pinned on the left-hand side of her white silk blouse and when she suddenly leaned forward it swung from her bosom like a pendulum.

'Kiss?'

She kissed him suddenly on the mouth. Her lips were most beautifully soft and full, not at all like the lips of Miss Flavell or his aunts, some of whom had hairs on their chins.

'That was nice,' she said. 'I liked that.' Everybody started laughing because now he darted forward and gave her a second kiss. 'Thank you. I liked that even better. When do you think I shall see you again?'

'Thursday.'

'Oh! Oh!' his father said. 'Here! Here! – off to bed now – up Wooden Hill.'

'That's it,' she said. 'And down Sheet Lane. And play a game of Shut-Eyes.'

'Good-night,' he said.

'Good-night,' she said. 'See you Thursday.'

Then as he ran quickly out of the room he heard her say, in her northern accent, laughing at the same time:

'Well, that didn't take long. That was a conquest if you like. I've soon got myself a beau.'

He didn't know what either a conquest or a beau was, but as he lay upstairs, trying to get warm in the cold clean bed, he heard her singing for the first time. It was a round liquid voice and he did not wonder at all that next morning his father spoke of her as a bird.

'You know, there wasn't a tremor there. Never the ghost of a tremor there. That was singing if you like. There's nobody in this town can sing like that. It made Maggie Flavell look a bit odd at her once or twice, I tell you. I don't wonder they call her the Pemberton Thrush.'

'I don't think she looks much like a thrush,' he said.

'Well, you should know!' his father said. 'You were the one who got closest to her.'

'She's nice,' he said. 'I like her.'

'That girl knows *how* to sing,' his father said. 'And I tell you something else – her words. You can hear every jack one of them. I tell you, that's before your time.'

Whenever his father said something was before your time you knew that it was very wonderful.

After that, all through that winter, she was at the house twice a week, sometimes three times, for practices. He looked forward to the time when he could go in to say good-night to her, kiss her and take part in a little game they played together.

It was a game about her watch. It started because he wanted to know, one evening, how you opened it. 'Inquisitive! Inquisitive!' his father said, but she said 'Let the boy be inquisitive. That's all right. That's how he'll find out things.'

You opened the watch by a tiny secret spring. It took him several weeks to find it. As time went on he knew that his father was rather annoyed about it all, but it was always she who said:

'Well, now. Are we going to try to find how the watch opens? It's easy really. It's like everything else – easy when you know how.'

'You open it for me.'

'Oh, no,' she said. 'That's cheating. You open it and find out what's inside.'

'What is inside?'

'Ah,' she said. 'That's it.'

Then after he had said good-night he would lie upstairs in bed and listen to the sound of her singing. He could pick out her voice, warmer, deeper and more flowing than all the rest. Once there was deep snow on the ground and bitter frost that made the ice on the pavements crunch as hard and crisp as the sugar you got out of candied peel. He did not know whether it was the purer, sharper air of the snow-world that made her voice seem more melting that night but she sang, he thought, with exceptional depth and beauty. It was like someone singing with all her heart and her flesh. The voice seemed to drive with its melting cadences far through the still night-world of ice and snow.

He was still not asleep when they finished singing. The footsteps of the three singers who were going home crunched hard on the icy pavement outside. Then he got suddenly out of bed and pulled back a corner of the blind and looked down at the street below.

Miss Flavell was already crossing the street and going away alone. Frost was like stiff icing sugar on all the roofs of the street, shining in the light of the street-lamp and the stars. Miss Flavell's high lace-up boots kicked powder snow as they ran.

He heard Miss Mortenson laughing. Mr Welsh whispered something and laughed too. He thought she laughed rather in the way that she sang: warm in her throat, with all her heart and her flesh, freely and very pleasantly and as if she loved laughing.

Then Mr Welsh was pressing her against the railings of the garden fence below. Her hat was knocked back on her head. Trying to save it, she brought both hands up above her head and gently put the hat in its place again. Then for a moment or two the tips of her fingers stayed together, not locking but simply touching lightly, and then gradually fell apart. It was during this time that Mr Welsh was kissing her.

Some days afterwards the snow melted; it was not long before spring came. The evenings became lighter and he thought it was not so nice to go into the front parlour and see no fire there and no candles burning on the piano.

Then a strange thing happened. One spring evening he

went into the front parlour to say good-night and she was not there.

'Isn't Miss Mortenson here?' he said. 'Where is Miss Mortenson?'

'Inquisitive, inquisitive,' his father said. 'Never mind about that.'

As he went out of the room, disappointed because he thought he had, at long last, discovered the secret of the watch, he heard his father say:

'Well, shall we start running through? She's bound to be here soon.'

'Well, we can only hope so,' Miss Flavell said.

Several evenings later he was alone for a time in the house when the door-bell rang. When he went to answer it Miss Mortenson was there.

'Is your father in?'

'No. He's gone to chapel with mother, to practise for Easter.'

'Perhaps I could come in and wait?' she said.

'Yes,' he said.

He was glad about that. He took her into the front parlour. She was wearing a pretty, flouncy white blouse with big puff-sleeves and a blue skirt with a black patent leather belt, and on her blouse the watch was pinned.

'I think I know how to open your watch now.'

'You do? How?'

'Like this.'

He turned the watch in his hands. On the back of it was a periwinkle flower, in blue, with trailing stems. She had said to him once 'Perhaps if you tried to pick the flower –' and then he had thought it out. At the very tip of one of the trailing stems was a little spring.

You touched it and the watch came open.

'There! You got it at last,' she said. 'All this time.'

'And what's inside it?'

'Ah,' she said.

He opened the watch more fully and sat looking inside.

'A lady,' he said. 'You.'

'You think it looks like me?'

'Yes,' he said. 'Only your hair's much nicer now.'

He supposed it was for that that she kissed him. She laughed and said something about his knowing how to treat the ladies and say the right things to them. Her lips were as warm and shapely as ever and there was a wonderful scent of lily-of-the-valley at the neck of her blouse.

'Well, I must run along now,' she said. 'Give this to your father, would you?'

It was an envelope and he said he would give it to his father.

'I know you won't forget,' she said.

He promised he wouldn't forget.

'I'm glad I found out about the watch,' he said. 'Can I open it again on Thursday?'

'I shan't be coming on Thursday,' she said. 'I don't think I shall be coming any more.'

The trouble was, his father said, that she was too free. She was too friendly. He said this over and over again during the next week or two. He said several more things and seemed agitated and affronted and even pained as he said them.

'She sang at the Band Club on Sunday,' he said. '*At the*

Band Club. Think of that. A girl like her. A voice like that. R.J. told me.'

Whenever his father said he had been told things by 'R.J.' or 'F.W.' he knew that it meant that little pigs had big ears and he was not supposed to be listening. It was always some terribly serious thing; very secret and not very nice, if he said he had heard it from 'R.J.'.

'Too free,' his father said. 'Spoiled herself. With that voice – with a voice like that' – behind it all lay some ghastly, inexcusable disappointment. 'I don't know which is the worst, club or pub. Singing on Sundays. Cheap concerts. Cheap low-down concerts.'

His father began by being upset and then was distressed and angry.

'And you know who's at the bottom of it, don't you? Jerry Latham.'

'Never was any good,' his mother said.

'She met him up north somewhere. At some competition where they were both singing. I say singing – he never could sing. That's why she came down here. He talked her into it. And I suppose she was fool enough to listen.'

'Always something oily about him,' his mother said. 'Never anything but a masher.'

'When I think of a voice like that,' was all his father could say. 'Wasted – completely wasted – thrown away.'

How, the boy thought, could anyone be too free and too friendly? A nice warm person like that. What did that mean?

'Too fond of attention,' his father said once. 'Too easily led. Too ready to give and too ready to take – and she doesn't mind who from. You know what P.S. told me yesterday?'

'I wish Miss Mortenson would come again,' he said.

'You speak when you're spoken to,' his father said. 'Never mind about Miss Mortenson.'

He did not, in fact, see her again for thirty years. Then after a visit to his father he was travelling down to the main-line junction one winter afternoon, through fields of snow, across the valley where his father and Miss Flavell and Mr Welsh and the Pemberton Thrush had so often gone to soirées and socials and concerts and competitions to sing songs like *On the Banks of Allan Water* and *Drink to me only with Thine Eyes* and *Have you seen but a white lyly grow?*

He did not recognize her at first. She sat in the corner of the railway carriage, bunched up in a brown fur coat. Even when she said, in her easy Northern accent: 'Enough to freeze you, isn't it? They never have any heat on this branch-line. And if there's anything I do hate it's snow,' he was still not quite sure of her.

Then he saw her bring the tips of her fingers together, either in a gesture of impatience or annoyance at the cold, the wretched branch-line or the snow, and he saw at the same time the watch on her wrist. It was the same watch he had so often tried to open as a boy. She had had it made into a wrist-watch with an expanding bracelet of silver.

'I don't suppose you would remember me,' he said.

'No,' she said. 'I don't know that I do.'

He told her his name.

'Oh! Lord,' she said.

Her hair was still dark but the smooth skin of her face, once taut and full, had now a deflated sort of look and was yellow.

'Don't tell me that,' she said. 'That takes me back too far.'

Her laugh was rather cracked.

'Do you still sing?' he said.

'Me? Oh! lord no,' she said. 'I gave that up in the First World War.'

'You had a fine voice,' he said. 'My father thought the world of it.'

'Oh! don't talk about it,' she said. 'It takes me back too far.'

His memories of her were so vivid that each time she made a gesture, either with her head or her hands, he felt that he was back again in the front parlour of his father's house, in the cold blue-flamed winters of his childhood, entranced by the candles on the piano, by her voice and the periwinkle watch he could not open.

He was tempted several times to ask her about the watch. He was tempted also to ask her why, with a voice like that, she had given up her singing. But he felt that perhaps the first question was rather silly and he did not know how to frame the second. All he said was:

'My father still sings a bit. It keeps him going.'

'I know,' she said, 'but then your father's not a fool.'

Almost unintentionally, without knowing it, she tugged at the lapels of her fur coat in a gesture of impatience. Behind the impatience there was a look of remote sadness in her eyes that, he thought, was not of her making. She coughed. The fur coat did not suit her. It was not quite that he expected moths to fly out of it but simply that it made her look like an old brown-haired, shapeless, moulting dog.

'Some people are too daft to know they're alive,' she said.

He felt he would like to have told her that she was pretty too; but it was not easy, in a railway carriage, before almost a strange person, to re-frame and re-state an impression of childhood so that it carried the right air of truth. Perhaps, he thought, she had not been quite so pretty as that? Perhaps she had not really been able to sing so beautifully after all?

'I could have gone with the Carl Rosa,' she said. 'But then, I tell you – some people are too daft to know they were born.'

'Well,' he said, 'I can tell you this. You gave one person a great deal of pleasure.'

'That's something at any rate.'

Abruptly, with her newspaper, she rubbed at the half-frozen vapour of the carriage window and stared out at the snow.

'If you ask me there's more of this stuff to come,' she said. 'The papers say there's snow all over Europe. You bet we'll get it if they do.'

She shuddered and pulled the fur coat about her.

'You know what I'd like to do with myself when the snow comes?' she said. 'Bury myself.'

It was perhaps ridiculous, but when she said that he was aware of tears inside himself. She pulled back the floppy sleeve of her coat and looked at her watch. There was evidently something wrong with it and she shook it several times and put it to her ear.

'This damn train's running late again,' she said, 'or else it's my watch. It's like me – getting past it. What do you make the time?'

'The time?' he said. He looked at his own watch. 'I make it exactly three minutes past.'

'We ought to have been in ten minutes ago,' she said. 'Now I'll miss my connexion.'

'Don't worry. They always wait,' he said.

'That's all you know.'

She hugged on to her lap a large black string bag stuffed with all sorts of oddments. 'What a day to be out,' she said, 'what a day to be alive.'

The last he saw of her was when she made a scrambling sort of run down the station platform, over frozen snow, panting to catch the main line train. Her body was too short for a fur coat of that kind and again he thought she looked like a shapeless, moulting dog.

Even before she got into the carriage snow began to fall again. He actually saw a few big fat flakes settle on her moulting fur. Soon all the air was dancing. And as he watched it he remembered her hands holding her hat in the snow, the nights when she had stooped to kiss him, the periwinkle watch whose spring he could not find and her voice singing with such warm dark beauty in the winter night-times.

'Bury yourself,' he thought. 'Someone will weep for you.'

'You were dead the time before last,' he said. 'Why don't you stay dead?'

He aimed for the third time down the straight grey barrel of his ash-stick, fixing the black point of a bud like a sight on the face of the girl sitting among pale green masses of curving bracken frond. He had shot her, the first time, between the eyes. He knew that that had killed her. Now she had turned her face away. It was a rather pale delicate face, with short bobbed hair, almost white, airy and separated as thistledown, and he aimed at the shell of her ear.

The sound he made of a bullet going through woodland was something like the high thin note of a tuning fork. He made it with tight-pressed lips, as if he were blowing up a difficult balloon. After it he made noises of grating savagery in his throat. Then he closed one eye, opening it at last to the thinnest crack that revealed slowly the brown bright watchful seed of a pupil squinting down the ash-barrel to the bud, and then beyond the bud to the bullet hole.

At this moment the little girl turned and looked him full in the face, slowly too, with eyes so transparent that they were almost colourless.

'Are you ready?' she said.

'You're dead,' he said. 'You've been dead three times already. You ought to lie down. You can't be dead so many times.'

'I don't like being dead. I don't like being killed all the time.'

'That's what we're playing,' he said. 'Being dead.'

'You're not,' she said.

'I'm playing ambushes,' he said. 'You're the one that's dead.'

He looked at her for some moments longer with puzzled exasperation and then came out, shouldering his ash-stick, from where he had been lying behind a hawthorn bush. A hawthorn bush was the nearest thing he could find to an ambush, which he supposed was also something that grew.

'We can't kill each other now,' he said. 'We're not playing for a minute. We're having a truce.'

He climbed the fence into the orchard. The fence was very rotten and in places no longer a boundary between woodland and the orchard of old, dying cherry trees, moss-grown and tilted, under which bracken was making its invasion in crooked fronds.

'Let's play houses,' the girl said.

They had played houses the day before yesterday and she had liked it very much. The house was in the bracken and there was a kitchen where they ate their meals. The saucepans were old tins from the dump in the wood and in one saucepan they had cherries and in another bunches of elderflower, which were really cauliflower with cheese on top.

'We'll play wounded,' he said. 'I'll be wounded and you can bandage me.'

'I like houses,' the girl said.

'Wounding and killing's more fun,' he said. 'I'll be wounded.'

74

'How will you be wounded?' she said. 'Who's going to wound you? Am I?'

'No,' he said. 'I get wounded in the jungle, out there.' He made brave off-hand gestures in the direction of the woodland. 'I'll get wounded and crawl out and you hear me groaning.'

He began to retreat in attitudes of stealth through the bracken, crawling under the lowest wire of rotting fence. He was an inch or two taller than the girl and his brown eyes, bright again after the cloud of exasperation, turned from beyond the fence and looked through the middle wires, fixing her with a sort of pained truculence.

'You have to play properly,' he said.

She sat gazing at her bare feet with unsure, unwilling eyes. She had taken off her shoes because, in the ambush, she was supposed to be a native and natives, he said, never wore shoes.

'All right,' she said.

'When you see me you shriek and start tearing up your petticoat.'

'Do I shriek if I'm a nurse?' she said.

'You're not a nurse. There aren't any nurses out here. It's too wild. You're my wife,' he said.

When he finally disappeared beyond the fence, into an undergrowth of hazel and elderberry and fern, the girl looked for some moments in the direction of the sounds he made. The sudden dying of dry squirrel-like rustlings among fallen leaves left the air filled with the dead calm of summer, the stillness so deep that when suddenly the wood was split with the shrieking squawk of a blackbird she was terribly startled and sprang to her feet and began screaming too.

'Oh! my dear, my dear, my dear,' she said. She ran with her small hands wringing themselves above the pale thistle-bob of her hair, her voice wailing in a tiny rabbit-scream.

Almost immediately he emerged from the wood with downcast arms, plunged into a desperate tiredness.

'They haven't started to shoot me yet,' he said. 'I haven't had to fight yet.'

'Did I start too soon?'

He fixed his eyes on her with slow, withering adultness.

'You don't see me until I come out of the wood,' he said. 'Then you start screaming. Then you run and hold me up and all that.'

'I'd rather play houses.'

'I'm going home,' he said.

He threw down his ash-stick and her eyes became immensely round and wet, a painful blue under pale, damp, almost invisible lashes.

'Don't go home yet,' she said.

'You never play right,' he said. 'You always muck the whole thing up.'

'I didn't muck it up when we played houses,' she said. 'There was a blackie and I thought it was you. I'll play right this time.'

He made a slight upward gesture of his arms, suspending in mid-expression what seemed to be a great patient and difficult sigh.

'All right, this once,' he said. 'You wait till I get to the fence, then scream.'

'Can I be in the house getting dinner?'

'All right, you be in the house getting dinner.'

'What shall I get?' she said. 'Steak and kidney and cauliflower with cheese on top like we had?'

'No. Lamb!' he said. 'Steak and kidney, steak and kidney, steak and kidney – all I get is steak and kidney. How do you expect a man to live and work on that? I want lamb today – lamb with red gravy.'

'I'll make mint sauce too, shall I?' she said.

'Good-oh! Plenty of sauce and gravy,' he said. 'Well, I'll be going now – goodbye!'

'Goodbye, dear,' she said.

In the house of bracken she cooked, on two bricks, a length of cherry-bough, making mint sauce of grass. From time to time she straightened the curtains at the windows of bracken and peered happily and delicately out, neat and efficient and no longer dreamy, to the world of woodland and summer and cherry trees.

The meal was almost cooked and she was waiting for the first groans of the wounded when she heard, from across the orchard, the laughing yell of another voice. Slowly she came out of the bracken house and saw, running down between the cherry trees, a girl in a red dress, with two red hair ribbons flying from dark brown plaited hair.

Excitedly the running girl began to wave her hands. The girl beside the small house of bracken did not answer. She watched in silence the running eager figure coming down through the cherry trees and then suddenly the air was nipped with the sound of shot, again like the ting! of a tuning fork. The running girl gave a strange high cry and lifted her hands and then fell, a second later, dead under the cherry tree.

Presently the boy came nonchalantly out of the wood, the ash-gun under his arm, his lips big, spitting at air.

Casually he turned the red dress over and looked briefly down at the stark-eyed face.

'She's dead all right,' he said. 'I got her.'

And then:

'Janey, you're dead.'

'How can she speak if she's dead?' the fair-haired child said. 'The lamb and mint sauce is ready.'

He ignored lamb and mint sauce and put the toe of one shoe under the waist of the girl in the red dress, gently kicking her.

'She can if I say so. Janey! you're dead. You can get up now.'

When Janey got up, smiling, her brown hair, with its dark firm plaits, gave her an air of confidence and certainty. It did not seem possible, as with the fairer, smaller child, to see her suddenly and lightly blown away.

'That was the most wonderful fall down dead I ever saw,' the boy said.

'Shall we have dinner now?' the fair child said. 'Let's have dinner.'

'Did I do it right?'

'It was marvellously marvellously marvellous,' he said

'What are we playing?'

'We're going to have lamb and mint sauce and red gravy,' the small child began to say, but the boy said:

'Ambushes. That's the ambush over there.'

'Can I play? Can I be ambushed?'

'I think the meal will get cold if we don't have it,' the small child said. 'You know how lamb gets cold.'

'I'm in the ambush and you come along the road here. You can fire back if you like. I fire first because I'm behind the ambush. Then you fire back and we have a battle.'

'Do I get killed?'

'You get killed in the end,' he said, 'and I get wounded.'

'I'm going to tear up my petticoat,' the small child said.

But the boy was already running for the wood, making renewed and now more ferocious noises of savagery in his throat and turning at the fence to say:

'It's a Sten-gun now. Not an ordinary gun. It fires all the time.'

'I'm going to tear up my petticoat,' the small girl said.

The dark girl gave a quick scarlet swing of her plaits. 'They don't tear up petticoats now. It's old-fashioned. Sometimes they tear up sheets but not petticoats.'

'Tom said petticoats.'

'They don't tear up petticoats, do they, Tom?'

'No,' he said. 'That's daft.'

'I'll be in the house,' the small girl said. 'I'll be keeping the lamb warm.'

As she crouched down, hiding herself with quietness in the house of bracken, the red flash of dress and hairbows ran up the slope of the orchard with a whine of jeep-sounds.

For a few moments afterwards the air was silent, only the breath of summer making a slow stir in high boughs of oak and cherry. The sky seemed to be filled with pale blue milk and among the rising bracken the thistle-head of the girl, not ruffled, was shining and white as silk in the sun.

Suddenly the jeep came down the slope and a second or two later the Sten-gun was firing with bright stutters from behind the hawthorn. The scarlet dress rolled in the road, over and over, and then straightened on its face, muttering strenuous resistance, firing back. Sometimes the girl yelled in her excitement and once the boy shouted back:

'I give you one more chance. I'm giving you one more chance and then I use tear-gas,' and for a second she lifted her head and before she could lower it again the Sten-gun beat her to pieces.

She was still dead in the road, eyes flat to the sky, when the boy came over and said:

'That was a trap, Janey. That's how I got you. When I said about the tear-gas it was a trap.'

'I know,' she said.

'I'll see if I can trap you again,' he said. 'Some other way.'

'What about dinner?' the small child said. 'Let's have dinner.'

'We don't want dinner,' the dark girl said. 'You're always talking about dinner. Why don't you shut up about dinner? If you don't want to play go home.'

'I was here first,' the small one said. 'I was here before you.'

'What difference does that make?' she said. 'It doesn't make any difference, does it, Tom?'

'No,' he said.

'There you are – Tom says so.'

'You don't even know how to fall down dead,' Tom said.

This time, as the battle began, she did not go into the house of bracken, with its cooling lamb and mint sauce of grass and the cauliflower with cheese sauce on top that now looked, in its rusty tin, like nothing so much as squashed sprays of elder-flower.

She did not look much at the battle either. She knew it was a very good battle because the shots from the wood never stopped and once there was a bang, preceded by a long whistle, that was a bomb. At the end of it the girl with the scarlet dress was dead again and she and Tom were lying together in the grass, rolling about, laughing excitedly.

'Come on. Again,' Tom said. 'I blew the jeep to bits. This time you're a convoy.'

'No,' she said. 'This time I'll ambush you.'

'No. I'm the ambush. I'm the man. I have to be the ambush.'

'No,' she said. 'I want to be the ambush this time.'

The boy seemed to hesitate. He seemed very slightly bewildered by the slow warm character of her smile.

'I'll let you kill me just the same,' she said.

Her brown eyes held him for a moment fully and now the expression on her lips was only a half-smile.

'Good-oh!' he said. 'Come on.'

'Aren't we going to play houses? With dinner?' the fair child said.

'No. Not now. We don't want to,' he said. 'You go home.'

She did not speak. Presently she walked away up the

slope of orchard, under the cherry trees, in a series of stops and starts, like a piece of slow-blown thistle-down now and then gently stopped in its progress by blades of grass. At the top of the slope she paused to look back. Under the cherry tree, where the house was, the sound of battle was dying away and she saw the girl climbing out of the ambush through the wires of the fence to the road where the boy was standing with his arms held over his head, in surrender.

She stood staring at all this for some time longer. She had forgotten her shoes and now she dared not go back for them. Her eyes were big and colourless. One of her small stony lips was held tight above the other and it might have been that she wished, after all, that she too was dead.

A Great Day for Bonzo

THAT July morning when we lay in the corn-loft where the martins were nesting it was so hot and quiet that every breath of chaff-dust falling through the floor-cracks looked like a puff of smoke as it drifted to the stable below. There were just the three of us, myself, Janey and Biff, the boy from the butcher's, lying as still as death on the floor-boards and staring through them to where, in the stable, we could see a man knotting a rope with his hands.

'He's making a lasso,' Janey whispered.

'That's not a lasso,' I said. 'It's a halter. It's like my grandfather goes to fetch the horse with.'

'No. It's a lasso,' she whispered. 'I know it's a lasso.'

Biff, the only one who didn't speak because he had enough to do keeping the martin's eggs safe in his cap, always wore the same big brown cap, with a proper peak, like a man's, and it was just right for putting eggs in. He couldn't see much either because he hadn't got his glasses. Whenever he climbed trees or barn-roofs or hedges to look for nests Janey and I always had to hold his glasses for him in case he broke them. Without them his eyes looked funny, not only boss-eyed, but naked somehow, as if they had peeled.

Janey was still holding his glasses while the man got busy with the rope and all Biff could do was to lie there groping with his hands and trying to squint with his boss-eyes at what was happening below. I think I really liked Biff so much because he was boss-eyed. It made him look funny and friendly at the same time. He was a wonderful tree-climber too and one day, when we were grown up, we were going round the world together, and afterwards Janey was going to marry one of us. Neither of us knew which one and nor, at the time, did she. Sometimes I thought it would be Biff because he was the best tree-climber and then sometimes I thought it wouldn't because he was boss-eyed.

Presently the man undid the big slip-knot he had made and then made another and pulled it tighter. After that he hung the rope over his shoulder. Then he looked up. That was the first time I ever saw his face and it made me very surprised. It was a kind, nice face, I thought, but it had a dark savage bruise under one cheek-bone and it looked thin and tired. His hair was short and grey and his chin the colour of pumice stone and his moustache was the same kind as my grandfather's. It curled out and then hung loosely down and I remember wondering if, like my grandfather's did, it ever got into his tea.

After he had looked up he took the rope off his shoulder and then started to sling it over a cross-beam. I couldn't think why he wanted to throw it over the cross-beam. It wasn't very easy to see all that was happening in the stable because the door was closed and the windows were hung with old bits of harness and horse-collars with frayed check linings and an old tin lantern with a lump of staring candle inside.

I think he threw the rope up three or four times before he realized the beam was too high. After that I saw him walk up and down the stable several times, trying to find another place.

After about a minute he came to the manger. Above the manger were wooden racks for hay. One of the racks had an iron ring in it and I saw him look up at it for a time. Then he climbed on to the manger, balanced himself on it and then started to thread the rope through the ring.

I began to wish I wasn't there. My throat felt tight and parched. I think Janey began to wish she wasn't there too because suddenly she started whimpering. I don't think Biff was frightened because he still couldn't see very well. All he did was to grope about on the floor, knocking chaff-dust through the cracks and not knowing it was puffing out in little clouds.

About half a minute later the man had the rope tied to the ring. He gave it a hard wrench or two with his hands. Then he did a thing that made my throat feel tighter and more parched than ever and I wished again I wasn't there.

He suddenly put the rope round his neck and then turned away from the wall and shut his eyes. By that time I was getting frightened. I didn't like to see him there with his eyes shut, his legs crouching a little, just as if he was going to jump off the manger on to the floor below.

Janey was already whimpering again and I was ready to cry myself when suddenly, from outside the stable, a dog started barking and scratching madly at the door. For some minutes I had heard something making thin shrill sounds out there but I thought it was simply the sound that house-martins make when they fly backwards and forwards or sit and talk to each other in the summer-time.

As soon as he heard the dog barking the man stood bolt upright again. He snatched the rope from his neck and started yelling.

'Go on, damn you! Git off – go on, damn you, git off back!'

I think the dog must have leapt as high as the top of the stable door when it heard the voice of the man calling to it from inside. I heard its claws slide down the wood-work, scratching madly. It howled too with that terrible moaning wail that dogs give when they're trapped or tied up too long or unhappy. When the man shouted again it made no difference. The dog wailed and leapt higher than ever at hearing his voice and it was even worse to hear it the second time because there was a sort of overjoyed panic in the way it was fighting to get in.

Then the dog hurled itself bodily against the door. I heard its skull actually hit the bottom of the door and then it was scratching madly, trying to tear a hole in the bricks of the step.

The man jumped down from the manger. He jumped down so suddenly that I had forgotten the rope was still not round his neck and I think Janey and Biff had too. Janey started crying openly and Biff stumbled to his feet, scraping the floor-boards and sending a mass of chaff-dust through the cracks in bigger clouds.

When the man saw the dust he stopped suddenly and looked up. His face was dead white now and more drawn. Outside the door the dog was still howling and scratching and whimpering and the man seemed undecided for a moment whether to let the dog in or come to us upstairs.

He let the dog in. It flew at him, wailing. Then it went round and round in circles, rolling on the floor. It was a small white dog, a cross between a wire-haired terrier and something else, and it had brown-black marks on the side of its face that were very like the bruise on the face of the man.

'Down,' he said. 'Git down! Damn you – how did you git out?'

The dog lay on the stable floor. Its pale pink tongue was like a piece of quivering india-rubber. As it cowered there I thought for a moment the man would kick it but instead he made a heavy, loose sort of gesture with one hand, trying to calm it. That was the first time I noticed how big his hands were. They were so big that they looked sadly naked and helpless, more naked and helpless than Biff did without his glasses, and he said:

'Down, boy. Down. All right, boy, quiet now.'

A moment later he started to come up the wooden stairs to the stable loft. I began to think of the eggs in Biff's cap. I knew that none of us ought to have been there and I felt sick and started shaking.

At the top of the stairs was a trap-door. We hadn't come in that way because it was more fun to climb the wall of the bullock-yard outside and then push each other up and get through the window. None of us knew that the trap-door was there and the sudden sight of the floor-boards opening and the man's big grey head coming up through it made Janey give a little yelp, something like that of the dog.

'Who are you kids? What are you up to?' the man said. 'Come on down. Come on – come on down.'

Biff was the first to go down, with Janey following him and saying 'Biff, wait for your glasses. Here's your glasses, Biff,' and then to the man: 'Don't you hit him will you? He can't see very well without his glasses.'

The funny thing now was that Janey was calmer than either of us. She was the shortest of the three, even smaller than I was, although I was the youngest, but she was thick and sturdy, with dark brown hair made into two short pig-tails tied with thin white ribbon and bright dark eyes.

'Don't you hit him,' she said. 'He can't see very well. If you hit him I'll tell the policeman.'

Then Janey gave Biff his glasses back and he started to huff on them, in the way he always did before he cleaned them up, and I noticed he stood aside. I knew then that he was only afraid of being hit because of the eggs in his cap. At the same time I knew I was afraid of everything, more than afraid: I was terrified about the eggs, the thought of the policeman, the man who stood there so white and tired, with his huge helpless hands, and even of the dog.

'You kids no business up there,' he said. 'You know that. What were you doing up there?'

'Nothing,' I said. I was sick and trembling. 'Nothing.'

'Up to no good,' he said, 'I'll bet. Up to no good.'

'We were studying birds,' Janey said. 'We have to study birds.'

'Birds' nesting, eh?' he said. 'Pinching eggs? Trespassing? The policeman can get told about that as well.'

'If you tell the policeman I shall tell the policeman,' Janey said. 'I shall tell him what you were doing up there.'

She pointed to the manger. The rope still dangled from the hook. We all looked at it, the man more drawn-faced than ever, alert and startled. I wasn't sure if Janey knew what the rope was for. I wasn't very sure myself. But the sudden way she pointed at it, her mouth tight, her little pig-tails stiffened out and her eyes as bright as black marbles, all at once created in the man a strange change of attitude.

'Here,' he said. 'Here. I'll tell you what.'

His voice had become soft and husky. All its tiredness seemed to rise to the surface of his throat in an enormous indrawn sigh. At the same time he bent down, snapped his fingers and thumb together and called the dog. It came over to him almost sliding on its belly. In its exhaustion it looked even wearier than he did himself and at last it lay down in front of him, its head on its paws, panting.

'Like him? You go on home now and you can have him. I'm going to part with him,' he said.

We stood in front of him with open mouths. Biff had his glasses on again and now they looked like moons.

'Go on,' he said. 'Take him. Call him Bonzo. That's his name.'

At the sound of his name the dog lifted his head.

'You want a bit of string on his collar, so you can lead him,' he said, 'that's all.'

'Bonzo! Bonzo!' Biff said.

The dog leapt to his feet, tail up, his tongue quivering, and from that moment I was no longer so afraid.

We were about a quarter of a mile down the road, going past the pond where we always found moorhens' nests on the fallen branch of willow, when Biff said he thought it was his turn to lead the dog. Up to that time Janey had been leading him. We had arranged to lead him in turns, each having him five minutes, with me taking the second turn because I was the smallest one. We had no idea of time but Biff said the best thing was to change over every time we counted five hundred. Neither Janey nor I could count up to five hundred and nor, in fact, could Biff. But he could count up to one hundred, he said, and do it in one minute, which meant that it was five minutes every time he counted a hundred five times.

We were just standing by the pond, arguing about whose turn it was, with Biff saying he wouldn't get the dog a bone from the shop if I didn't let him take second turn, when suddenly the dog gave a snatch with his head, whipped the string from Janey's hand and started back up the road.

We all ran after him and were about a hundred yards behind him when he reached the bullock-yard. At one time there had been a farmhouse on the far side of the yard. Now it wasn't a house any longer but was used instead as a barn for storing straw. The windows never had any glass in them and straw stuck out of the holes in the same way as it does out of the holes in a scarecrow.

Now too there were only bullocks in the yard in winter and never any horses in the stables except perhaps at hay-time or harvest when a man put his team there at dinner time because it was the coolest place in the heat of the day.

So as we ran across the yard to the stable beyond the only moving things about the place were ourselves, the dog and the house-martins flying high in the sun. Just outside the stable stood a big sycamore and the shade of it was so black that the dog, flashing under it all doubled up with excitement, looked like a rolling snowball.

Biff could always climb trees better than I could, but he was on the fat side and I could run much faster. Janey was always bold and clever but she couldn't run at all. So I was first across the bullock-yard and first under the syca-more and the dog himself wasn't so very far ahead of me as I reached the open stable door.

I don't know what I expected inside the stable but when I reached the stable door I stopped. It was terribly quiet inside and the stable seemed to be empty. The shade of the sycamore helped to make it dark too and my eyes, coming out of the brilliant morning sun, were dazzled.

Then I heard the dog. He seemed to be somewhere far inside the stable, towards the end of the manger, and he was whimpering. I started calling 'Bonzo! Bonzo!' and then I went inside.

Suddenly I saw the dog crouching in the shadows be-hind the staircase that went up to the loft and beside him was the man. He was just sitting on the floor with his big hands flat on his knees, staring in front of him.

'He got away,' I said. 'He broke the string and we couldn't stop him. We couldn't help it. Is it all right to have him back?'

He didn't answer. There was a funny look on his face and I felt he hardly knew I was there. I remembered see-ing much the same look on the face of Miss Burgess, who lived alone in the street next to us, the day a black van came and took her away.

Just at that moment Janey and Biff came in, both of them shouting 'Bonzo! Bonzo!' and then stopping suddenly, just as I had done, because it was dark inside and their eyes were dazzled.

'Come on, Bonzo,' I said, 'come on, boy,' and I reached out to take him by the collar.

He started to back away. He didn't exactly show his teeth but his lips stretched like a catapult and quivered back again.

'Where is he?' Biff shouted.

'He's here,' I said. 'He won't come with me.'

Then Janey and Biff came up to where I stood, watching the man and the dog.

'I'll make him come,' Biff said and he started to say 'Bone – big bone, Bonzo – fat bone – me find big bone, Bonzo. Come on, Bonzo,' but the dog stretched his lips again and backed away.

'Why won't he come?' Janey said.

She was talking to the man but again he didn't move or answer.

'Doesn't he know you said we could have him?' she said.

'Perhaps he didn't hear you say,' I said. 'Perhaps you ought to tell him again.'

'Bone, Bonzo,' Biff said. 'Big bone, Bonzo.'

Slowly, after a moment or two, the man raised his head. He had been simply staring straight in front of him, cold and glassy, as if none of us were there.

'Where do you kids come from?' he said. 'Where do you live I mean?'

'We all live in the same street,' Janey said. 'Biff and me live opposite each other. Biff lives at the butcher's shop. His father's the butcher.'

'I work at the butcher's sometimes too,' I said. 'Saturdays. Making sausages. I turn the handle of the sausage machine while Biff puts the meat in.'

'We brought our dinner out for the day,' Biff said, 'but we've eaten it.'

The man seemed to think about this. His mouth fell open a little as he sat thinking and once he put one of his big hands up to his cheek, touching the bruise on it gently.

'Butcher's?' That was all he said, but I know he hardly knew what we were talking about. He spoke the word very slowly, like someone who couldn't spell or pronounce properly, and then went on staring again, unaware of either us or the dog.

'You tell him,' I said. 'You tell him and he'll come.'

'Yes, you tell him,' Janey said.

'We're going to lead him five minutes each,' I said. 'Then each one's going to keep him a week at a time.'

Once again he raised his head. Every time he raised his head the dog looked up, always slowly but somehow sharply, fixing his eyes on him. It was a very curious thing, but I got the impression, each time, that the dog knew what the man was thinking.

'Here, boy,' he said and I thought at first he was talking to the dog. But then I saw that he was speaking to Biff. 'He might come better if you went and got that bone.'

'All right,' Biff said. 'All right.'

'Bring it with some meat on it,' the man said, 'if you can. And a bit o' bread too. He likes a bit o' bread.'

'Janey's uncle sells milk,' I said. 'Does he like milk?'

'Dogs never eat milk,' Biff said. 'Cats eat milk. Dogs eat bones and bread.'

'We had a little dog once and he ate milk,' Janey said. 'I could get some milk if he eats it.'

'He eats it,' the man said. 'He eats anything. What sort of sausages have you got?'

'We don't have sausages Tuesdays,' Biff said. 'We have polonies though. And scratchings.'

'He likes scratchings,' the man said. 'You bring him a bit o' polony and a few scratchings and he'll do anything for you.'

'Will he beg?' Janey said.

'He'll beg. You'll see,' he said. 'You got to make friends with him first though.'

'We'll go,' Janey said to me. 'You stay here.'

I started to feel a little frightened again at the thought of being left alone there with the man staring so oddly in front of him and the dog who seemed to be able to read his thoughts and I said:

'Doesn't he like cake? My mother could give me a piece of cake if he likes it. Caraway. We had some on Sunday.'

'He don't like cake much,' he said.

A moment later Janey and Biff started to run out of the stable and I was all alone with the dog and the man and there was no sound except his heavy breathing as he stared in front of him and the thin whistle of the house-martins across the yard outside.

We sat for a long time alone together, not speaking. Once I remembered the rope and looked round and saw it still hanging by the hook above the manger. But for most of the time I sat staring through the open stable door, out to the black pool of sycamore shade and beyond it to where morning sunlight burned down on big green bunches of elderberry, part of a rusty hay-drag and an occasional swooping bird.

I wasn't really frightened; his face was too kind for that; I only wished that Janey and Biff wouldn't be gone too long and that sometimes the man would talk to me instead of staring in front of his big loose hands.

I thought of several things to try to make him talk but at first he either never answered them or wasn't interested.

'Do you play jacks?' I said.

'Play what?'

'Jacks,' I said. 'Jack-stones. You have five stones – Janey plays. She's better than anybody. She can do all-ups and grabs and anything. Can you?'

He didn't answer again; I could see he wasn't interested in jack-stones.

'Where do you live?' I said.

He didn't answer that either. I saw a martin come down and settle on the wall against the elderberry tree, his tail quivering dark in the sun. I watched him until he flew up again, snapping at something in the hot still air, and then I thought of something else to say.

'Have you got a horse?' I said.

Whether he had a horse or not I never knew.

'My grandfather's got a horse,' I said. 'A white one. We had another white one before that but it wasn't well and we had to shoot it. Then they came and took it away and made currant jelly of its hooves.'

Sometimes the dog stirred but mostly, when the man was quiet, the dog was quiet too, lying on its belly, motionless, its head on its paws.

'Do you like Janey?' I said.

He wanted to know who Janey was and I told him, explaining at the same time:

'She's either going to marry me or Biff. I don't know which yet. We shall have to wait and see.'

Suddenly, for the first time, he turned on me quite fiercely.

'Married?' he said. 'Don't you have nothing to do with that caper.'

He must have seen that I looked quite startled at his fierceness because abruptly his face altered. It seemed to lighten and broaden and suddenly, to my enormous relief and surprise, I saw him smile.

A moment later he actually turned and laughed at me.

'What was that you said about horse's hooves?' he said. 'What sort o' jelly?'

'Currant.'

'God alive,' he said, 'currant?' He even laughed a second time. 'You sure it wasn't apple or summat?'

'No: currant,' I said. 'Red. Like you have with hare.'

That seemed to put him in a much better humour and I said:

'Which do you like best? Hare or rabbit? I like hare. My grandfather catches hares with a bit of string and a wire and a bit of stick in the hedgerows.'

'Never?' he said.

I was thinking up something else to say when he laughed outright again. It almost seemed as if the dog was laughing too and while he was still in that state of good humour I decided to ask him something that had been troubling me for a long time.

'What were you going to do with the rope?' I said.

He went back at once into his brooding, uneasy, groping stare, not answering, and again I felt terribly sorry for him because of his huge helpless hands.

'You weren't going to lasso yourself, were you?' I said.

His voice was suddenly short and fierce again.

'You keep your mouth shut about that,' he said. 'Keep your mouth shut.'

He spat on the floor as straight as you shoot out of a pea-shooter and then stared at the blob of spittle for a long time, again as if I wasn't there.

'You never see me up there, did you?' he said.

I started to say I had seen him up there.

'No you never,' he said. 'You never see me.'

I was going to say a second time that I had seen him but he shook his head slowly and said:

'No you never. You never see me and you ain't never goin' to tell nobody you did. Are you now?'

'No,' I said.

'What you don't see you can't talk about, can you?' he said.

'No,' I said.

'If you don't tell it nobody can't hear it, can they?'

'No,' I said.

'That's right,' he said.

We sat for a little while longer, not talking much, and then I said:

'Shall I go and find some jack-stones? Then Janey can show you how to play when she comes back.'

What I really wanted was the chance to get outside to see if there was a sign of Biff and Janey coming back and I was glad when he said:

'That's it. You go out and find your jack-stones. And see if you can find a little tin or summat and a drop o' water and bring the dog a drink while you're there.'

I went outside. It was hot and still in the sun. From the top bar of the gate in the bullock-yard I stood and looked across the fields and the road for a sign of Biff and Janey. The road and the fields were empty. In the distances, above the hedgerows, across the flat blue-green ears of corn, waves of heat were shimmering and dancing just like water.

Then I got over the gate and began to look in the cart-track for jack-stones. Already the track was hard and baked from summer and bits of blue chicory were flowering in the disused cart-ruts, with a lot of silver-weed and shell-pink sunshades. Where the track was barer I found five stones, one almost a pure white one, about the size of a robin's egg, and then three brown ones and a bluey-grey one with red veins in it, all scribbled about, just like a writing-lark's.

Then I got back over the gate and went round behind the building that used to be a house but was now a straw-barn. An old gas-tarred water-barrel stood under the eave, by the doorway, and in the nettles beside it I found an old enamel saucepan, blue outside and white inside, with a hole in it that had been plugged up with a piece of sack.

I climbed up on the barrel and looked down at the water. It was very black and about half-way up the barrel and I could see tiny red worms in it, wriggling like hairs. I started to try to catch the worms in the saucepan and at the same time I could see my face, with its smooth, almost white hair, reflected in the blackness of the water below.

I've no idea now how long I was fishing there in the water-barrel; I lost count of time. But suddenly, side by side, with the reflection of my face in the water, there was his face. It seemed suddenly to fall out of the sky and float there without a sound.

'Give us that,' he said. 'I'm as dry as a fish,' and he took the saucepan from me and started drinking.

I was too surprised and startled to be frightened. His big gloomy face staring up at me out of that black water-barrel froze the back of my neck. I wanted to start running. I actually slipped down the side of the barrel, catching my bare knee in one of the hoops, and in another second or two I should have been away, my legs melting, across the fields.

Then I saw him drinking. He was drinking like a horse, his mouth and most of the front of his face buried in the saucepan. He made a sucking desperate sound just like a horse and after he had emptied the saucepan once he filled it a second time and then a third.

What fascinated and terrified me about all this was the thought of the worms. I knew you should never drink water out of water-barrels. If you did the worms would grow inside you and swell up and poison you and make you die. I knew there were three sure ways you could die. One was by not eating; the other was by not breathing; and the third was through drinking water out of water-barrels where there were worms.

When he had finished his third saucepan of water I looked up and stared at him and said:

'You'll die, drinking that water. The worms will swell up inside you and you'll die and they'll put you in the bury-hole.'

That was the worst thing I could imagine, being put in the bury-hole. That was the most terrible, awful thing in the world, I thought, but he didn't seem either impressed or frightened.

'That wouldn't come amiss, would it? Not to some folks. Not to me, chance it.'

'You don't want to die, do you?' I said.

'Die?' he said. 'Very like they'll come a time when you'll want to die.'

'No,' I said. 'No.'

'Ah! but you never know, do you?' he said. 'That's it. You never know.'

I was too puzzled to answer. On his wet, stubbly face the sun shone down fierce and brilliant, making the skin seem glassy and jagged. He actually started to take another drink of water. Then he changed his mind and doused the rest of the water over his face, wiping it off with big swabbing jabs of his coat-sleeve.

'Where's the dog?' I said. I suddenly remembered the dog. 'Where's Bonzo?'

'Tied him up,' he said. 'We got to take him some water.'

He dipped another saucepan of water from the barrel.

'Why do you want to give him away?' I said.

'He's nothing but a plague to me,' he said. 'He plagues me to death. I'll be glad and thankful to be shut on him.'

'He's a nice dog.'

'He's all right. He plagues me though. I wish he was somewhere.'

We took the saucepan of water and started to walk back to the stable.

'Soon as them other kids get back you can hop it,' he said, 'and give me a minute's peace. You can take him with you and I'll get some peace for a change.'

The dog was tied up at the foot of the stairs. When we gave him the water he lapped at it without stopping for breath. 'Drier n' me,' the man said and I was just beginning to feel dry myself and wondering whether I should quench my thirst by sucking one of the pebbles, like my grandfather did in the harvest field, when I heard the voices of Biff and Janey coming back across the yard.

For a few seconds I thought the eyes of the man would drop out of his head when he saw what Biff had brought.

'That's all right,' he kept saying. 'That's good.'

Biff had brought a shin-bone of beef, a red polony sausage, and a good big handful of scratchings, all wrapped in newspaper. Janey had nearly a pint of milk in a can. In one pocket Biff had a pork pie wrapped in grease-proof paper and in the other three rounds of bread.

He unwrapped the shin-bone first and then started to spread the newspaper on the floor, but the man grabbed it out of his hand.

'That ain't today's, is it?' he said.

He began to peer at the newspaper, his eyes bulging and close to the page. There were still beads of moisture on his face but I couldn't tell if they were sweat or water. His big hands made the pages crackle as he turned them over and then suddenly he folded the paper up and gave it back to Biff.

'Yesterday's, ain't it? Yesterday's,' he said. 'What's the date there?'

'The twenty-ninth,' Bill said. 'That's the day before.'

'Twenty-ninth,' he said. He sat thinking, again in the same huge, helpless groping way as when we had first seen him. 'Twenty-ninth – what day are we now?'

'Tuesday,' Janey said. 'We told you before.'

'Tuesday, eh? What date was Saturday?'

'Twenty-sixth,' Janey said.

Janey was always quicker than any of us but that time I was quick too.

'Have you been here all that time?' I said.

'Get the grub out, get the grub out,' he said.

He picked up the shin-bone. For a moment I thought he would start gnawing and tearing it with his hands. By now the dog was on its feet, straining at the string that still tied him to the stairs.

'Here, Bonzo, Bone. Bone,' Biff said and the dog started whimpering. 'Come on, boy – bone. Here boy, here –'

As the dog gave a great straining pull at the string, rushing forward and then choking himself back, whimpering again, the man raised the shin-bone with a menacing swing and said:

'Don't start harbourin' him in bad habits. Git back there! – go on, git back.'

'He's got to have the bone, hasn't he?' Biff said.

'All right,' the man said, 'but not all of a minute. The bone's to get him to go with you, ain't it? That's what you brought it for.'

It must have been past midday by that time. As Biff started to unwrap the pork pie I began to feel hungry. We had eaten our dinner at half-past ten and I think Biff and Janey were hungry too. Biff started to get out his shut-knife, ready to cut the pie, but the man said:

'Hold hard a minute. What are you cutting that for?'

'It's for us,' Biff said.

'What about me? Don't I git no dinner?'

'If you like,' Biff said. 'You can have some polony if you like.'

He grabbed the polony, tearing the top skin off with his teeth. Then he held it in his fist like a big scarlet ice-cream cone, gnawing and licking the sausage out of the top of it. Biff held out a slice of bread and he grabbed that too. All the time he never spoke a word. Once or twice the red skin of the sausage got gnawed loose but it made no difference to him: he tore it with his teeth and ate that too.

'You can have some milk if you like,' Janey said.

With his mouth full of sausage he buried his face in the milk-can, drinking out of it in the same sucking, slopping way as he had drunk water from the saucepan in the yard.

'How are the scratchings?' he said. He began to eat the scratchings, throwing them into his mouth, then crunching them like nuts. Scratchings are the bits of pork leaf you get left over when lard is made. They're a brown-golden colour and crisp and they're better with salt on them. I thought perhaps he would ask for salt but it never seemed to occur to him as he threw the scratchings into his mouth and crunched them madly down.

'What about the dog?' I said suddenly. Everybody had forgotten the dog. 'I thought we got the scratchings for Bonzo.'

He threw a few scratchings on the stable floor, not speaking. The dog went for them as madly as he had done, licking the floor for crumbs.

'What about the bone?' Biff said. 'Can't he have the bone?'

'Lotta meat on that bone,' the man said.

It was true there were skinny bits of meat with a few bluish sinews left on the bone, but I hardly thought he would eat them. Then I heard his teeth grate on the bone, gnawing at flesh. It made queer cold shivers run across the small of my neck to see a man eating raw meat like a dog and once more I felt sorry for him and I know by the way Biff and Janey sat there staring, forgetting the bread and the pork pie, that they were sorry too.

Suddenly, for the first time, he seemed to become really aware of us sitting there. His eyes rolled about for a few seconds, white and big and watery. He spat up a piece of gristle that had got caught in his throat. This seemed to wake him still more and after he'd taken another drink of milk he said:

'You kids can bunk off now. Tie the string tight round your hand this time so he don't git loose. It's no use if you don't tie him tight. He'll only git loose again.'

'Like a piece of pie?' Biff said. I think we were all a little sick at the thought of the pie. After seeing him tear the flesh from the bone like that we none of us had much heart for the pie. 'You can have some if you want to.'

He started wolfing the pie. Sometimes a piece of the crust, with trembling bits of jelly, fell out of his hands or his mouth on to the floor below but again it made no difference. He always picked it up, cramming it into his mouth without wiping the dirt from it or even bothering to look at it at all.

'Anybody down the road when you come back?' he said suddenly to Biff.

'No. Nobody,' Biff said.

'There was a man across a field hoeing wezzles,' Janey said.

'One says yes, one says no,' he said. 'Make up your minds.'

'There was a man,' Janey said, 'but he was right across the field.'

'All right, all right,' he said, 'If he's there when you go back don't say nothing – don't talk to him. If he sees you just look slippy.'

'All right,' we said.

He was still finishing the pie and we were still sitting on the floor, staring at him, when I remembered something I wanted to ask him.

'You've got a big bruise on your face,' I said. 'Did you know? If you'd have thought of it Biff could have brought a piece of meat for it. A piece of meat on a bruise makes it better.'

To my surprise he completely ignored the question of the bruise. I might never have asked it. Instead he looked at each one of us in turn and then said:

'Who's going to lead him this time?'

'It's my turn,' Biff said.

'Who led him last time?'

'Janey started.'

'All right. You lead him,' he said to Biff. 'Now git hold of him tight. No half-larks. And one on you walk in front with the bone. Who's going to walk with the bone?'

'I want to,' I said.

'All right,' he said, 'you walk in front of him with the bone. Then he'll follow you till bull's noon. All you got to do is keep in front with the bone.'

'I will,' I said.

By the time we left he was lying down on the stable-floor staring upward.

'Now perhaps I can git a minute's peace,' he said. 'Perhaps I can git some peace now.'

Outside, across the bullock-yard and down the cart-track where I had found the jack-stones, it was hotter than ever. The sun was straight and blinding. A few thistles were already seeding by the hedgerow but there was hardly a breath of air to blow the down away.

When we got to the gate leading out to the road we stopped a moment and something made me get up on to the top bar of the gate and look back along the cart-track, with its blue stars of chicory and sunshades in the sun and tufts of bearded thistledown to where, by the syca-more, the stone walls of the stable were almost white in the sun.

'He's come out to watch us,' I said.

From the gate we could see him at the door of the

stable, looking round. The queer thing was that, after all, he did not seem to be looking at us. He reminded me of someone who was looking round for intruders, just to satisfy himself before locking up a house, for the last time, at night.

Suddenly he disappeared. A second later we all heard the big bolt of the stable door slam back inside. In the hot still air it was like the sound of a rifle bolt being snapped in, hard and steely, in readiness to fire.

The dog, I thought, seemed to have heard it too. Almost at once he started whimpering and scratching under the lowest bar of the gate, trying to get through.

'Start running with the bone,' Biff said. 'Give him a smell of the bone and then start running.'

We got him about three hundred yards beyond the pond, almost to the point where the road forks, about a mile from the town, when he suddenly doubled back, wrapped the string round Biff's legs and started back up the road.

At that moment I was ten yards or so ahead with the bone and as soon as I saw him turn I turned too and began to run after him. I realized at once that I should never catch up with him, and the only way I could think of stopping him was to throw the bone.

I threw it as hard as I could and it bounced behind him with a thump on a pile of stones at the side of the road. As soon as he heard it fall he stopped, turned and made a grab for it. The bone was nearly as big as he was and it looked like a big red table-leg as he stood there on top of the pile of stones, wagging his tail and looking for the first time very pleased with himself and very sharp and cheeky.

'Drop it! Drop it!' I said.

'Shut up!' Biff said. 'Now he's got the bone he'll come as easy as pie. Won't you, Bonzo? You'll come now, won't you?' He started slapping his knees with his hands and looking appealingly at Bonzo through his big moon spectacles, at the same time approaching him gently, calling his name and sometimes whistling. 'Come on Bonzo boy. Come on, boy, come on –'

The dog actually dropped the bone on top of the pile of stones and then stood with his mouth open and his tongue out, laughing.

'Good boy, Bonzo,' Biff said. 'That's a boy –'

He suddenly rushed forward to grab his collar but in a second Bonzo picked the bone up and dived back into the tall grasses along the roadside and then through a blackthorn hedge and into the field beyond.

At that point the blackthorn hedge was too thick and prickly for the three of us to get through but there was a gate thirty or forty yards up the road and in a few seconds we were climbing over it into the field. The oats growing right up to the gate and the hedgerow were twice as tall as us and were a soft pink-yellow colour, ripe for cutting. There was no sign of the dog. I watched for the oat-stalks to start moving but nothing stirred and there was no sound except the sound of grasshoppers whirring in the heat of noon and a yellow-hammer singing the same few notes over and over again on another side of the field.

'Bonzo! Bonzo!'

We called him over and over again but he made no answer. I got on my knees and tried to look through the rows of oat-stalks but on the headland they were running the wrong way and it was like looking into a forest of pink-yellow straw all tangled with thistle stalks, pink convolvulus and little flowers of scarlet pimpernel.

Then Janey, who was always so quick, thought she heard him farther down the hedgerow. We all listened and I thought I heard him too, panting softly.

'Let's track him,' Biff said. 'Get down. Start tracking.'

We started to go off in Indian file down the hedgerow. Biff leading, Janey next and I coming on behind. Every few yards we stopped, crouched down and listened. Sometimes there was a sudden faint stirring down the rows of oat-stalks but it never went on for long and it might have been only a rabbit, or field-mouse or a bird.

'He must be in the other field,' I said. 'Let's look in that.'

'I know where he is,' Janey said. 'He's gone back to the barn.'

'No,' Biff said, 'he's in here, I know he is, I can smell the bone.' He turned round from where he was crawling on his hands and knees and looked back at us with his funny eyes that always seemed to be swimming out of one side of his thick watery spectacles and said: 'You can smell it. You smell. You can smell the bone.'

For a minute we all stopped and smelled. Perhaps Biff was more used to the smell of meat than I was but I couldn't smell anything except the ripe oats, the seeds of grasses and the clay earth turned dry and dusty by days of sun.

'I can't smell anything either,' Janey said. 'I'll go back to the barn if you like and see if he's there.'

'No,' Biff said. 'I can smell it. It's over there.'

I suppose we had crawled about a quarter of the way round the field before, as we stopped for the tenth or eleventh time, we heard another sound. It was a harsh, crisp, swishing sound, regular and steady, and neither Biff nor Janey knew what it was.

But I knew what it was.

'It's a man with a scythe,' I said. 'He's mowing round the field.'

All three of us lay down in the grass by the hedgerow, listening, not daring to breathe. Then after a few moments I moved over towards the oats and parted some of them with my hands and looked down the rows. The rows were very straight there and this time they ran parallel with the hedgerows so that, some distance down them, I could actually see the scythe swinging and biting into them and just behind them the trouser legs of the man, his boots summer-dusty, the legs of the trousers tied up with bits of string.

Suddenly the man stopped mowing. I saw the blade of his scythe flash white as he laid it down on the stubble. Then he moved away and I could not see him for a moment or two but presently I heard him spit once or twice and after that there was a sound of water trickling by the hedgerow. Biff started laughing into his hands and then I saw the man come back. He laid his jacket on the last swathe of oats he had mown and then sat down on it and began to unpack his dinner, a lump of bread-and-cheese, some onions and a big blue can of tea, from out of a round straw dinner bag. Before he started to eat he spread his handkerchief on his knees and took out a big clasp-knife and wiped it on his trousers. The handle of the knife was thick crinkly bone and the handkerchief was red with big white spots on.

All that time none of us dare move and then, down the rows and a little to the left, between myself and the man, I caught sight of something else.

It was Bonzo, lying in the rows of oats with his feet on the bone. As soon as I saw him I was so excited that I forgot everything else: the man, Janey and Biff, where we were and how we were not supposed to be there and what might happen to us if we were found. I was so excited that before I could stop myself I was calling him by his name.

'Bonzo!' I said. 'Bonzo –'

I hadn't called him more than twice before he bolted. He went straight forward, crashing through three or four yards of oats and then leaping clean past the man eating his dinner on the stubble beyond.

The man let out a yell as the dog leapt past him and I think he was more frightened than we were as we turned and started running. The last I saw of him was a glimpse of his brown bald head as he snatched off his cap and threw it at the dog.

A moment or two later we were crashing through a gap in the hedgerow, out into a pasture field beyond and skulking and scurrying down the ditch like terrified leverets, panting for breath.

When we reached the road there was no sign of Bonzo. You could see the empty white curve of the road quivering at each end with shimmering waves of heat and again there was no sound in the hot midday air but the whirr of grasshopper and the short tinkling song of yellow-hammers along the hedgerows.

'He must have gone across the fields,' Biff said. 'That way.'

'I bet he didn't,' Janey said. 'I bet he went to the barn. He *wants* to go to the barn – can't you see? – that's where he *wants* to go.'

Biff thought the field and Janey thought the barn. I couldn't make up my mind where he would go. I was really thinking about the man with the scythe and how he would probably chase us. All I really wanted was to be able to find the dog, take him back home and start making a kennel for him and teach him to fetch stones, but Biff said:

'All right. I'll go across the field and look and Janey go to the barn and look. And you,' he said to me, 'stop here.'

'I don't want to stop here –'

'You stop here,' he said. 'You guard the road. You be sentry.'

I didn't want to be sentry. I was five and a half, but Janey was six and a half and Biff was over seven. Whenever there were things they felt I was too young to do they always made me sentry.

'You sit on top of the stones and keep your eyes skinned,' Biff said.

'And if he comes,' Janey said, 'catch him and hold him by the collar and tie him to a tree.'

I don't know why, but I felt uneasy and queer as soon as Janey went up the road and I hadn't been sitting long on the pile of stones before I began to wish we had never let her go back there all alone. Somehow I couldn't get out of my head the picture of the man with the rope, how he had drunk the water with worms in it and eaten raw meat off the bone and how, above all, he just sat there with his uneasy groping stare and his enormous helpless hands.

'Janey,' I thought, 'if you're not back soon I'll count a hundred and if you're not back then I'll come and look for you.'

I don't know how long I sat on the pile of stones all by myself, between the high blackthorn hedges that already had their little grey-green sloes on them, in the hot still sun, waiting for Janey and Biff to come back. All the time there was no sign of Bonzo and once I started to play jack-stones, but after a time I gave it up because the stones were too big for my hands. Then I began looking among the bigger stones, turning them over, and finally I found a long flat one that had a lot of wonderful things underneath it: a rain-beetle, a lot of pigs that rolled themselves up in balls, a devil's coach-horse and a big fat brown slug that I thought at first was a toad.

Then I started to count up to a hundred because Janey wasn't back. I couldn't really count up to a hundred. I could only count up to twenty and then, as I always did at hide-and-seek, skip and pretend the rest.

'*Twenty*. One, two three – *thirty*. One, two, three, four, five – *fifty*. Fif-one, fif-two, fif-three – *seventy*. Nine-two, nine-three, nine-four, nine-five, nine-six, *a hundred*!'

I didn't know until afterwards that all the time I was sitting there playing with the stones, looking underneath them and pretending to count up to a hundred, something strange was happening to Janey in the stable.

When she got back to the stable the door was open. After a few moments she went inside and looked about her but neither Bonzo nor the man was there. Then she went outside and stood for a moment under the big sycamore, listening.

After a time she thought she heard a sound. It seemed to come from the direction of the building that had once been a farmhouse. She went across the bullock-yard towards the house and presently she saw the man standing by the water-barrel, muttering to himself.

'Have you seen the dog?' she said. 'Have you seen Bonzo? We've lost him again.'

He turned on her, startled. She told me afterwards how his eyes looked strange and green. I never really believed that. Nobody's eyes could ever look green, I thought, but I believed her when she said:

'Don't you remember how Arthur Burgess looked when he thought he'd eaten the poison-berries? He looked like that. He looked bad as if he was going to die.'

I knew what was really the matter with him. I knew that he was going to die because he'd drunk water with worms in it. That was a sure way to die, as sure as stopping breathing or not eating food. Anybody ought to know that was the way to die.

Then before she could say anything else he turned on her and said:

'You get outa here – go on, git out on it. Allus vapourin' round, you kids – git out on it. Leave me be.'

'We want Bonzo,' she said. 'I think he came back here. Did he come back?'

He didn't answer. She said he seemed to go faint suddenly and gave a big shiver, standing there in the sun. His face was terribly pale, she said, and the bristles on his face stood out like stiff grey prickles.

Then he started to wander back towards the stable, groping his way. She followed him, saying a few things, asking questions, mostly about Bonzo, which he never answered.

At last he was in the stable and once more he lay down on the floor. He lay with his face away from her for a time, muttering, half-speaking things with little groans. She sat down on the floor beside him, sorry for him, and asked him several times if he felt bad and once if he wanted water.

At the mention of water he turned and looked at her as if he were seeing her there for the first time.

'Do you go to school?' he said.

'Yes,' she said.

'Why ain't you at school today?'

'We just started holidays,' she said.

He stared at the stable floor and then got himself up on one elbow and said:

'Can you write?'

'Yes, I can write,' she said. 'I'm nearly seven. Miss Jackson says I'm a good writer.'

He didn't speak for a time. Instead he fumbled in his pockets until finally he brought out a stub of pencil and then a piece of paper.

'You know where Blackland Spinneys are?' he said.

'Yes,' she said. 'We sometimes go primrosing there.'

He started to give her the piece of paper and the pencil as if he were going to ask her to write something down. But suddenly he changed his mind and put them back in his pocket. It was hard to know what he meant by these sudden changes of mind but it was harder still when he said:

'Do you read the Bible at school? Do you say prayers and all that?'

'Yes,' she said.

'Say something.'

She didn't know what he meant by that and she saw him lie back on the stable floor, flat on his back, with closed eyes.

'Say what?' she said.

'What you say at school.'

She had no idea what to say. The first thing that came into her head was *The Lord is my Shepherd*.

'Shall I say that?' she said.

'If you like,' he said. 'That'll do.'

'*The Lord is my Shepherd*,' she said. '*I shall not want. He maketh me to lie down in green pastures.*'

'God,' he said, once or twice. 'God. Oh! God.'

It was all a mystery to her. All the time she was talking she kept her eyes on his face. It was very quiet in the stable in the coldish shade, out of the sun, but she was never frightened. And the reason why she was never frightened, she told us afterwards, was because the strange, funny, cold-drawn look on his face gradually went away as she sat there. He lay quiet and tranquil, as if after a long and terrible tiredness he had started to drop to sleep.

116

He spoke to her in fact only once or twice more and then with his eyes still closed.

'Don't you come back here no more, you kids,' he said. 'Hear that? Don't you come back no more – I shan't be here.'

'Supposing Bonzo comes back?'

'He won't come back. He'll only come back if he knows I'm here. And I shan't be here. I'll be gone for good in a minute or two.'

She stood for a few moments longer before he finally asked her to go, saying, 'Shut the door.' Then as she stood at the stable door, just before shutting it, she remembered something.

'What about Blackland Spinneys?' she said. 'Is that where you live?'

He didn't answer.

'Do you feel better now?' she said.

He didn't answer that either.

'Thank you for Bonzo,' she said.

By the time she came down the road again to where I was waiting on the pile of stones Biff had come back too. There was no sign of Bonzo.

Then when Janey began to tell us all that had happened in the stable and the bullock-yard, how the eyes of the man were green and how ill he looked, as if he were going to die, I began to get more and more excited.

'He's going to die!' I said. 'He's going to die. I saw him drinking the water with the worms in it. That's the way you get poisoned. That's the way you die.'

'Die?' Biff said. 'You're not sharp. You can't die from drinking water.'

'You can,' I said. 'You can. Water out of ditches. Water with worms in it.'

'Then,' Biff said, 'how is it dogs don't die? How is it birds don't die? They drink water out of ditches. How is it cows don't die? They drink water with newts in it. And frogs. How is it they don't die?'

'Sometimes they do.'

'Yes, but not next minute. They don't drop down dead next minute.'

'Let's go and catch newts,' Janey said. 'We can paddle too. It's hot.'

'We haven't got Bonzo,' Biff said, 'have we? We can't go without Bonzo.'

We sat there for a few minutes longer trying to decide what to do when suddenly a man pushed his head over the gate farther down the road and said:

'You kids! – is this your dog? I nearly cut him a-two – you want to get him killed? Why'n't you take him home and chain him up somewhere?'

It was the man with the scythe. He had Bonzo gripped tight by the collar.

'He's all covered in burrs and thistles,' the man said. 'Got one or two in his foot too I fancy. That'll stop him capering off too far. Now you just git off home and take him with you.'

As we went down the road we were all so happy that we forgot completely, for the first time, about the man in the stable. And this time too everything went right with Bonzo. Biff held him really tight by the string. And, as the man said, there were thistles in his foot and sticky burrs all over his body, so that he limped a bit, looking almost, I thought, like a plum-pudding dog.

He looked a little sorry for himself too, I thought, sometimes hopping on three legs and holding the other in the air. The thistles in his foot were just what we wanted. We knew, with them, that he couldn't run very far.

Just before we got home we stopped for a few moments by a stone-mason's yard to decide who should have Bonzo first and how long each should keep him. Under the stone-mason's shed two men were sawing a lump of white stone and the air was full of hot dry dust from the saw. When the men saw us standing there with the dog they suddenly stopped sawing and one of them, wiping his neck with a sweat-rag, looked at Bonzo and grinned.

'That's a bit of a clanger you got there,' he said, 'ain't it? What run up the entry?'

The second man laughed too and said:

'Sausages goin' t'ave black and white skins this week, Biff?' They both laughed then. 'Or is he goin' into the pigs' puddens?'

They both seemed to think that that was very funny, but none of us laughed and Biff said:

'He's our dog. He's all right.'

'So long as he ain't mine.' the second man said. He was the funniest of the two and he blew his nose with his fingers. 'Does he have fits?'

We said he didn't have fits; we said he was a good dog and could run fast and you could teach him to beg. But the men didn't seem impressed by this and the second one spat and laughed again and said:

'If he starts gittin' fits you feed him on pigeon's milk. That'll cure 'im.'

'Pigeons don't have milk,' Biff shouted. 'But donkeys do!'

After that the men didn't seem to want to talk any more. So presently we decided that Janey, because she was a girl, should have Bonzo first and keep him for one week from that very afternoon.

Janey's father worked on the railway. Sometimes he worked on night-shift. You went up to Janey's house by a brick entry where her mother hung out the washing on wet days and beyond the entry was an asphalt yard and then a little garden where her father grew rows of onions, big clumps of red and yellow dahlias and a few potatoes. When he wasn't working on day-shift Janey's father would sit in the middle of his garden, on a broken kitchen chair, in a tiny square of grass that he clipped with scissors, and stare at his plants with pride and wonder.

Sometimes he put his plants into flower-shows and that afternoon I thought he would explode when he saw Janey leading the dog down the ash-path between the onions and potatoes.

'Get that dog out of here!' he shouted. 'Who brought that in? Who let that out? Go on!' he yelled. 'Get out – get out of here!'

He began to pick up stones.

'He's ours,' Janey started to say. 'Biff's and mine and –'

'Take him back where he belongs!' her father bellowed. 'Get him out of here!'

After that we led him slowly across the street to our

house. I knew my mother didn't like dogs; I knew my father didn't like dogs either. But it was in my mind to ask if Bonzo could live with my grandfather, who was a very nice, genial, easy-going man who kept a little farm where, at threshing-time, thousands of rats came out from under corn-stacks. In another month or two it would be threshing-time and Bonzo would be able to kill the rats and soon everybody, like us, would know how wonderful he was.

In the house it was very hot, the blinds were drawn and my mother was asleep in the sitting-room.

I went out into the street again and told the truth to Biff and Janey. 'My mother's asleep,' I said. 'I daren't wake her.'

Biff was glad.

'My father likes dogs,' he said. 'We always had dogs. Once we had a dog called Blinder. He could see in the dark. We had a big rat in the cellar and it got into a corner and its eyes had red flames coming out of them but Blinder killed it.'

'My grandfather has rats too,' I said. 'They live in the corn-stacks. Bonzo'll kill them.'

'I bet he's a good ratter,' Biff said. 'My father'll like him if he's a good ratter.'

Janey and I stood outside the butcher's shop while Biff went into the shop with Bonzo. Blue and white striped awnings covered the windows of the shop and there was a queer faint sickly smell of meat in the hot air.

Biff's father was a fat stocky man with red cheeks and ears, a bluish bald head and a funny way of being nice to you one day and not speaking to you the next. My mother said it was the smell of the meat: it made him liverish. Sometimes if I helped in the shop, with Biff, he gave me pig's-tails. I liked pig's-tails. There isn't much meat on a pig's-tail but what little there is is very tasty. I was always overjoyed when I got a pig's-tail, just as I was always downcast, when, for days on end, Biff's father wouldn't speak to me. But that was how he was, my mother said. You never knew how the man was going to be, five minutes together. That was how butchers were: the smell of the meat made them moody and fat and tatchy.

'Well, look on his collar!' we heard Biff's father shouting. 'Haven't you got sense enough to look on his collar? He belongs to somebody, doesn't he? There must be a name on the collar!'

In another moment he came outside with Biff, dressed in his blue and white apron with the big steel hanging from his waist, dragging Bonzo by the scruff of the neck. I could see he was in one of his liverish tatchy moods. He was purplish-hot in the face and he almost lifted the dog off the ground as he dragged it on to the pavement and said:

'Here, what does it say there? What does it say on the collar?'

Biff squatted down and turned Bonzo's collar round and then read out:

'"*Bonzo. J. Slater. High Farm. Blacklands Spinneys. Evensford.*"'

'Well, now you know,' his father said. 'He belongs up at Blacklands. Take him back there.'

None of us knew what to say.

'Go on – take him back. He's strayed. Take him back there – or else down to the police station. One of the two

– but I don't want him here. I won't have a moocher like that about the place.'

We led him down the street. He was still limping from the thistle in his foot and I thought he looked tired and thirsty. I was getting a little tired and thirsty myself and Janey said:

'Perhaps my uncle would have him. He could help get the cows in.'

But it was no use: her uncle said dogs were bad for cows. They worried them something chronic; they made their milk go sour. But he was a friendly easy man and he gave us all a drink of milk from a churn. The milk was cool and fresh from standing all day on the stone flags of the dairy and we gave Bonzo a drink of water from a tap in the yard. Then Janey's uncle gave us a pear each. They were small honey pears, soft and yellow and very sweet, the first pears of the summer, and they were so nice that all of us ate the cores.

'You start off now and take him back,' Janey's uncle said. 'That's your best tip. You don't want a policeman to see you, do you?'

That was the last thing we wanted. We remembered what the man in the stable had said. Up to that time we hadn't thought much more about him but now Biff said:

'Perhaps we ought to take him back to the stable. Shall we?'

'He said we were never to go back there,' Janey said. 'Never. He wanted to get a little peace, he said, and we wasn't to go back.'

'All right,' Biff said. 'We'll have to take him back to this farm. At Blacklands.'

Then Janey remembered something. The word Black-lands reminded her of the time she had sat in the stable with the man and how he had taken a piece of paper and a stub of pencil from his pocket and had said to her suddenly: 'Can you write?' and then 'Do you know a place called Blacklands Spinneys?' as if he were going to ask her to write it down.

'It's the same place,' she said.

'All right,' Biff said. 'I expect that's his home. Let's go up there.'

After we had been walking some time – the way to the spinneys was all up-hill and the road was white with heat and we rested several times – I remembered something too.

'I wonder if he's dead yet,' I said.

'He can't die,' Biff said, 'not from drinking water. Act sharp – I told you.'

'Perhaps he'll die in the night,' I said. 'People always die in the night.'

'That they don't,' Biff said. 'I had an aunt what died at tea-time.'

'If you die,' I said, 'can you come alive again?'

'No,' Biff said. 'It's just like meat. Meat can't come alive again, can it? Nobody can come alive.'

'Jesus did,' Janey said.

Janey was always so quick and clever and this time Biff couldn't answer.

After that I couldn't make up my mind whether people could come alive again or not and I began to be worried by the thought of the man in the stable and what we had seen there. I wondered if he died whether, when we went to look for martin's nests again, we might not find him there, under the manger perhaps, where it was dark, still staring upward.

'I want to go home,' I said.

'Oh! don't be a kid,' Biff said. 'Don't be wet.'

'You catch hold of my hand,' Janey said. 'When we get to the farm we'll see some hens.'

I don't know why but perhaps it was the thought of the hens, as we began to walk in the shadow of the spinneys, where the road was like a thin white tunnel between thick hornbeam and hazel boughs, that began to comfort me. Gradually I forgot the thought of the man who might be lying dead under the manger, below the old horse-collars and the lamp with its staring candle, and once I said:

'I like hens. My grandmother's got a hen that talks.'

'Hens can't talk,' Biff said. 'How can they?'

'This one can,' I said. 'You give it maize and corn and it eats it and then starts talking.'

'Nobody can talk only people,' Biff said, 'can they, Janey?'

'Parrots can talk,' Janey said, 'and sometimes jackdaws.'

'Let's catch a jackdaw and see if it talks,' I said.

'Come on,' Biff said. 'Don't *drag*. When do you think we'll get there?'

Perhaps it was not more than a mile up that road, between the woods dark and thick with summer, the birds in them quiet in the still afternoon and the primrose leaves burned in the ditches by the heat of July, but the road was straight and white and hot and it seemed much further.

Once we came to a pond and we stopped for a few moments to let Bonzo drink in it. All round the pond were thin tall reeds like dark green spears, with a few bulrushes among them and pink sprays of willow-herb. On the far side stood a clump of elder-trees and it was shady there. Part of the water was thick with water-lilies and between the leaves little circles kept springing up and dying away.

'Look,' Janey said. 'Fish. Coming up to breathe.'

'Fish can't breathe,' Biff said. 'If they breathe they die.'

'No they don't,' Janey said. 'They have to have air like people.'

'You don't know anything,' Biff said.

'Nor do you,' Janey said. 'Boys don't know everything. They think they do.'

I thought it was nice by the water, with the tall cool reeds, the shade of the elder-trees, the flat shining water-lilies, the water with its little spreading circles and hardly a sound in the air but the dog lapping water as he drank at the edge of the pond.

'Let's stop and catch fish,' I said. 'Or else newts, or tadpoles.'

'It's too late for tadpoles,' Biff said. 'You don't know anything.'

'We'll stop and paddle when we come back,' Janey said, 'shall we?'

'It's too deep to paddle,' Biff said. 'We'd all get drownded.'

After a time we walked on again, slowly, tired now in the heat, even the dog flagging, and I was just beginning to wonder if we should ever get there and if Biff perhaps wasn't after all something like his father, moody and tatchy because the smell of the meat got into him, when suddenly Janey said:

'There's the house. There's the farm. There it is.'

We all stopped. The house stood in a clearing of the wood. It was a house that you might have thought had been a church at one time. Its windows were long and narrow and rounded at the top. In the half-circle at the top of the window the glass was blue and yellow, with sometimes a piece of green. The window frames were painted a dirty reddish-brown and over the front porch, which had sections of coloured glass in it too, fell drooping masses of ivy, like a dusty dark green rug hung out to dry. The house was built of brick and at the back of it were a few brick out-buildings, all of them roofed in corrugated iron that shone brown with rust in the sun. Underneath them stood bits of machinery, rusty too, with old barrows, a water-cart, a hay-rake and several cans and churns.

What made you think of a church too were four big yew-trees that flanked the path leading down to the road. I didn't like these trees; they made me feel unhappy. I didn't like the way the road ended just beyond them either, the white line of it cut off by a gate, and how the woods beyond it, dense and taller now, went on and on, unbroken.

'Let's go back,' I started to say and then I noticed something terribly strange about the dog.

'He's shamming dead,' I said.

The dog was lying flat on his side, with his eyes closed

and all four legs crooked and limp, as if he had broken them.

'Come on,' Biff said and began trying to pull him to his feet by the collar.

Bonzo didn't get up. All that happened was that Biff pulled him about a foot along the grass and then dropped him in the same position.

'Perhaps he's hurt,' I said. 'Perhaps it's the thistle in his foot.'

Even Biff didn't think that was silly and we spent some time trying to clean his feet of thistles. Each time we lifted a foot it dropped back again as if it was dead.

'Now you can come,' Biff said. 'You're all right now, Bonzo. Come on now – come on, boy.'

Biff pulled hard on the string in a sudden jerk and Bonzo actually got to his feet. A moment later he started to behave like a mule. He dug his hind legs into the grass and showed a thin slip of his teeth and hardened the muscles of his chest so that Biff couldn't drag him.

'Come on,' Biff said. 'You've got to come. Push him. Push him from behind.'

The first moment we pushed him he let out a growl. It was the first time he had growled at us all day. It was guttural and hard. I didn't like it. Then I remembered suddenly that if dogs bit you you went mad and then you died.

'He won't bite us, will he?' I said.

'Not if you're not *frit* of him,' Biff said. 'If you're frit he'll bite you. He knows you're not master if you're frit. You've got to be master. Come on, Bonzo. I'll show you who's master.'

Biff went on for about another five minutes trying to

show Bonzo who was master. It was very hot trying to lug Bonzo to his feet and soon Biff's eyes began to look more and more like jelly beans and his glasses were misty with sweat. All the time Bonzo dug his legs into the grass, like a mule, and wouldn't budge. Once or twice he let out another growl and once he lay down again, his feet crooked and stiff and his eyes closed.

Then Janey tried with him. She lifted one of the lids of his eyes and peered into it. 'Why won't you come, Bonzo?' she said. 'Bonzo, look at me,' but she might have been peering into an empty buttonhole.

'We'll just have to go in and tell the people we've got him out here,' she said.

'Who's going?' Biff said.

'You go,' Janey said.

'I've done all the pulling and tugging,' Biff said. 'You go.'

'You're the biggest,' she said.

I was suddenly afraid they would send me because I was the smallest and I began to feel cold in my neck, my hair tingling like little watch springs.

'I'm fagged out,' Biff said. 'I want to lay down and get my puff back.'

'If somebody doesn't tell them we'll have to go to the police station,' Janey said.

'Don't let's go to the police station,' I said. 'You know what the man said.'

'They might lock us up,' Janey said. 'They might say we stole the dog.'

That seemed to impress Biff and he started hesitating. After he had hesitated a moment or two Janey said:

'Go on, Biff. You're the bravest. You always are.'

I think Biff liked that. He didn't look half so fagged out after that and he said:

'I've got to clean my specs first though. You hold him tight while I clean my specs.'

Then he took off his glasses and huffed on them and started polishing them on his handkerchief, sometimes squinting through them, so that he looked funnier and more boss-eyed than ever. I thought he spent a little more time on his glasses than usual and sometimes you might have thought he was a soldier, polishing his kit before going on parade.

Then he stood up. He pulled his big brown cap lower over his eyes and said:

'Hold on to him hard. Both of you. One of you take his collar and the other hold the string.'

'All right,' we said and we crouched down low in the grasses, holding Bonzo down.

Then Biff walked down the road to the house. I was glad I didn't have to go to that house, with its queer churchy windows, the black yew trees that made me unhappy and the way it seemed to stand neglected and isolated, in a gap in the woods, at a dead end.

When Biff got to the house he went round the back of it and knocked on the kitchen door. The farm-yard was empty. He told us afterwards he knocked three or four times and that no one answered. Then he thought he heard sounds from somewhere farther along that side of the house and he thought they seemed to come from an out-house, a wash-house or a dairy, at the end of the path.

He went along the path until he got to an open door.

It was in fact just a sort of out-house and inside it was a girl. She was sitting on a chair, plucking a chicken, and she was wearing a black pinafore.

Somehow, by the way she looked up at him, big-eyed and startled, he knew that she was frightened. He was half-frightened himself and he started to ask her if her name was Slater. As he said that she gave a sudden start, half-getting up from the chair, so that before she could prevent it the half-plucked chicken slipped from her lap and she just grabbed it in time, by one leg, before it fell to the floor.

'What made you ask that?' she said. 'Who are you? Where did you come from?'

'I've got your dog,' Biff said. 'I've got Bonzo.'

She stood up, still holding the chicken by its leg, loose and naked, at her side. She was a tall girl, with a lot of heavy black hair, and no colour in her face except brown smoky circles under her eyes. Biff thought she looked about nineteen or twenty. He couldn't tell. Perhaps she was more, perhaps twenty-five. He hadn't time to think much about things like that before she suddenly grabbed him and pulled him into the out-house and started jabbering questions.

'What made you think my name was Slater?' she said. 'Where did you find the dog?'

She jabbered so fast, her mouth loose and quivering, that he never got the break of a second to answer a single question until she had been talking for several minutes. Then she seemed to think of something. For a moment she actually stopped talking and looked out of the door quickly, up and down the yard.

Then he said: 'We got him from a man. In a barn. He said we could –'

'What barn? Where? What barn?'

She suddenly knelt down and gripped him by the hands.

'Tell me what barn. Where? Where is it? Tell me where it was.'

He began to try to tell her where it was but she interrupted him again, shaking him backwards and forwards nervously, her eyes big and close to his face.

'What was he like?' she said. 'Had he got grey hair? Were his hands big? What was he doing there?'

'He was acting funny,' Biff said.

'How? How do you mean? Where? How do you mean he was acting? – funny? How?'

Biff started to tell her how we had seen the man drink the barrel water and gnaw raw meat off the bone but again she didn't let him get very far. Again she smothered him with questions. Then at last she suddenly dropped the chicken on the chair and seized hold of his hands and said:

'Where did you say you had the dog? Where?'

'Just down the road,' he said. He hadn't told her before. She hadn't given him a chance and now he thought she would cry as he told her.

'How far down the road?' she said.

'A little way –'

'You go back,' she said. 'You go back now and start walking down the road. You start walking. Start walking, don't speak to anybody and in a minute I'll catch up with you.'

A moment later, and before he could move to go, she

was standing bolt upright. At the same time she made a grab for the chicken. She actually started plucking at it with her free hand, not looking at it. All the time she was staring at the doorway and when Biff turned he saw what she was looking at.

In the doorway was a man. He was tall too and thin, with straight black trousers held up by a belt. Biff took particular notice of the belt because it was like one his father used on him sometimes when the meat got into him and he was liverish and tatchy.

The man was slightly hump-shouldered too, in the sort of way that men get when they work on the land, stooping, and there was something peculiar about his eyes. Biff said he thought at first he was cock-eyed, like himself, and then he saw that the lid of one eye had been cut badly and hadn't healed properly, so that one side of it was screwed up by a dark scar, giving it a leer.

'Catch up?' he said. 'Catch up with who?'

She didn't answer. Her eyes looked frozen while her hands darted about the chicken, plucking it.

'Who's this?' the man said. His voice was hollow, crabby and grating. 'Who's he?'

Then before the girl could stop him Biff said:

'I brought a dog back. Is your name Slater?'

'Who?' The man turned on him sharply and swiftly. The shadow of an arm hooked over and the girl jabbered:

'Don't tell him nothing. Don't tell him nothing. Don't tell him.'

'What dog? What dog?' the man said. Biff tried to

step backwards out of the out-house but the man put his foot in the doorway and said: 'No you don't. What dog? Who sent you here?'

'Don't tell him!' the girl shouted.

'Shut your mouth!' he said to her. 'I'm talking –'

'Run,' she said. 'Run. You run now.'

'Nobody's running,' the man said. 'Not him and not you. The only one who's running ain't here and ain't likely to be –'

'Run,' she said. 'You run now.'

She made a sudden imploring gesture with her hands, forgetting the chicken. It slipped out of her grasp, falling to the floor.

Before she could move to pick it up the man stooped and grabbed it by the legs. For a moment Biff thought he would hit her with it. He actually swung it in the air and the girl actually put her hands to her face to protect herself, saying:

'You hit me. Go on. Hit me. You hit me again and see. You hit me once before – I thought you'd learnt that lesson –'

'I'm your father, ain't I?' he said. 'I ain't your father for nothing, am I?'

'You can hit me a thousand times,' she said, 'and it won't make no difference. I want him and I'll have him – chance what you say –'

He suddenly threw the chicken down on the table. She didn't flinch this time. She stood her ground, Biff said bolt upright, her eyes staring. The man made a guttural sound in his throat – it might have been that he was going to spit at her, Biff thought – and then he seemed to realize, for the first time, that Biff had heard all that was going on and he said:

'You git outa here. Go on. Make yourself scarce and don't come nosin' round folk's back-doors another time. Go on!' He started shouting suddenly. 'Go on –!'

Biff was frightened and started running. He hadn't gone more than half a dozen steps down the path before she sprang to the door and screamed after him:

'His name's Slater. That man – the man in the barn. Tell him it's all right – tell him to come here –'

'You tell him no such thing!' the man yelled 'Git out on it afore I limb you – you and the dog too!'

The girl broke free and started to run down the path. After a few paces the man caught up with her and after that all Biff could hear was his voice, shouting:

'He thought he'd killt me, didn't he? How many more times do I have to din it into you? It's all over and done with, I tell you, it's finished. Get that into your daft miserable head! Any more from you and I'll shoot you and him and the dog too.'

At the gate of the yard Biff's fingers were trembling so much that, for a moment, he couldn't undo the latch. And as he stood there trembling and fumbling he thought he recognized a familiar sound; the swish of a strap and the sound of a buckle beating.

I suppose we had been sitting by the pond for ten minutes or so, resting in the shade of the elder-trees, behind the thick tall lines of reed, when the dog began to behave queerly for the second time.

This time he didn't lie down and stiffen himself and

pretend to be dead. He suddenly stood up, looked in the direction of the woods and cocked his ears. Then his throat began to quiver, giving out a low rumble, like a toy dynamo. Then suddenly his tail went up and you could feel him bristling.

'I think he can smell a rabbit or something,' I said.

'He can *hear* something,' Biff said. All about us there was nothing but the deep soundless calm of afternoon, stretching far away through long woods, hot and without a breath of air. 'Dogs can hear things people can't. Listen!'

We lay and listened. With my face in the grass I held my breath, hearing nothing but the tiny whirr of insects in the heat, hidden somewhere among grass and reeds. Then suddenly I couldn't hold my breath any longer. I gulped and a puff of grass seed seemed to get into my mouth, so that I choked and started coughing.

'Shut up!' Biff said.

'I can't help it –'

'Shut up,' he whispered.

We lay for a few moments longer, listening. This time I lay on my side and the grasses looked like a gold forest, the tallest stalks like trees, the bits of totty-grass trembling like ferns above red-yellow tufts of egg-and-bacon flowers. There was still nothing I could hear except the click and whirr of insects about the pond and then Biff said:

'You keep hold of Bonzo. I'm going to look out on the road.'

We watched him squirm on his belly round the pond. He looked like an Indian tracking animals. As I watched him I wished I was an Indian too and we had a wigwam to sleep in, with Janey as our squaw. Then Biff disappeared behind a hawthorn bush and I couldn't see him for a time.

But presently I saw his face in the grasses, turning to come back to us. Whenever Biff was specially excited his spectacles slipped a bit – they were really always too big for him and sometimes he wound bits of wool round the bridge to keep them on his nose a little better – and his eyes started groping and getting bigger and bigger as they tried to look through the lenses and not over the top.

By the time he crawled back to us his spectacles were almost on the end of his nose.

'It's the man,' he said. 'The one from the house. He's coming down the road with a gun.'

As we all slipped down the bank and lay still further in the reeds I could still hear nothing but the sound of insects clicking and whirring in the hot afternoon. The dog had stopped his grumbling. Now we made him lie down too and Biff unbuttoned his jacket and wrapped it over his head.

After we had been lying there like that for a minute or two, the dog not moving now or making a sound, I began to hear the footsteps of the man coming down the road between the woods. The road was not more than ten or fifteen yards away from us and the footsteps were slow and shuffling on the dry loose stones.

It seemed hours before they stopped. All the time I was afraid I would start choking again and I kept my hands over my mouth, pressing my head against the hard clay bank of the pond and shutting my eyes. I opened them only once, just for a second, and I saw that Janey had her eyes closed too. But her lashes were quivering and she was biting her bottom lip hard on one side.

Soon the man started walking again. At first I couldn't tell if he was walking farther down the road or if he had turned now and was walking back again, towards the house. In the middle of wondering I thought of the house and how dark it was, with the big yews and the strange churchy-coloured windows, and how it seemed cut off from everywhere, isolated in the clearing of the woods, at the beginning of nowhere.

Then after a long time I couldn't hear the footsteps. It was not only quiet in the afternoon. The air was tingling everywhere and it made you tremble in your veins. At the same time I couldn't be sure if the man had walked away altogether or if he was still there, somewhere on the road, behind a hawthorn bush, watching and waiting for us to move.

I think we might have gone on lying there until darkness if it hadn't been, once again, for the dog. All of a sudden he struggled out from under Biff's jacket, stood on his feet and shook himself from head to foot with a shudder.

After that he went down to the edge of the pond and started drinking. The sound of him lapping the water was like somebody clapping their hands.

'Were you frit?' Biff said.

'No,' I said.

'No,' Janey said.

The three of us were lying there with him, at the foot of the bank, not drinking but dabbling our hands in cool water and then splashing it over our faces and our hair.

'I think Bonzo was a bit frit though,' Biff said.

'I wasn't frit until Bonzo was,' I said.

'Nor was I,' Janey said. 'I wasn't frit till he was.'

'Good old Bonz,' Biff said. 'Good old boy. Good Bonz.'

'What are we going to do with him now?' Janey said.

'That's it,' Biff said. 'What are we going to do with him? What are we going to do with you, Bonz, eh?'

Biff stroked Bonzo on the back of his neck. The dog took a last lap of the pond-water and then hopped up the bank and started to walk towards the road. Our faces and hands were still wet as we followed him.

'Where shall we take him?' Janey said.

'We'll stop at the end of the road,' Biff said, 'and have a pow-wow. You haven't tried your house, yet,' he said to me.

After that we took another look up the road, at the long dusty white slit of gravel narrowing away between parched summer woods, empty in the straight sunlight, and then started running.

We were still running, the dog in front of us, when about half a mile down the road a figure suddenly came running out of the woods to meet us.

It was the girl and she hadn't even washed the blood from her arms.

She was carrying a bag now, a sort of oil-cloth bag, black and shining, with a string handle, just like the one my grandmother used for bringing tea to us in the harvest field. You could see bits of clothing and newspaper sticking out of the top of it, as if she hadn't had time to pack it properly. She also had a comb in her free hand and two hair-pins in her mouth, but when she stopped she pushed the comb into the bag and started to fix the pins in her hair.

'Where's that man?' she said. 'The one you saw? The one you told me about? All right, Bonzo, all right. Down now, Bonzo, down.'

We started to tell her that the man was in the stable but the dog was so excited, whimpering and crying, jumping up against her skirt and twisting his body to and fro in excitement, that I don't know if she heard us or not.

All she said was: 'Could you take me there? Could you show it to me, please?' and she said this several times, still trying to fix the pins in her hair with one hand. Once or twice she looked back up the road but there was no sign of anyone there and Biff said:

'That man started coming. He was coming down there with a gun in his hands.'

'That's all right. That doesn't matter,' she said. 'You tell me where the other man was. Where was he?'

The dog was a little quieter by that time. She was able to hear what we said about the stable.

'You get to it by a track,' we said. 'Across fields. No-body lives there.'

'Take me,' she said. 'Show me, will you? Is there a short cut there?'

'We can go by the brook,' Janey said.

'There isn't a bridge that way,' I said.

'We can paddle over in the shallow place by the spring,' Biff said. 'Where the sticklebacks are.'

'Do we have to go through the town that way?' the girl said.

'No,' Biff said. 'No. Nowhere near the town.'

'That's good,' she said. 'That's good. I don't want to go near the town.'

Except that she had to stop once and put down the bag, and refix the pins in her hair because they had fallen loose again she hardly changed her pace as we went with her through the fields, by the short cut, along by the brook where we sometimes fished for sticklebacks and occasionally saw a kingfisher shooting down through the willow-herb and the reeds.

There was a kingfisher there that afternoon. It came swooping downstream in such a flash of blue and copper, crying thinly, that I was startled and Janey let out a little cry. But the girl either didn't see it or didn't give it a second thought if she did. She just kept walking, not so very fast, as it seemed, but with long strides, springing on her heels and swinging her long scarred arms. All the time her head was slightly down. Her thick hair kept falling into her neck and sometimes partly on to her shoulders.

At one of the stiles we had to climb she turned on us without really stopping and said:

'When did you first see him? How long ago was that?'

'In the morning,' Biff told her. 'A long time ago.'

You like some people the first time you see them, even if they're not very happy. I could see that she was not happy. I didn't know why, but her eyes were dark and the way she kept trying to pin up her hair was troubled and restless and queer. But I knew I liked her and because I liked her I felt there was something she ought to know.

'I think he'll be dead by now,' I said. 'I think he was going to die –'

'What makes you say that?' she said. She turned on me with big scared eyes, walking sideways, all twisted, her hair falling over one side of her face. 'Die? – why? – why would he die?'

'Because he drank water,' I said. 'Water with worms in it. Out of a barrel. If you do that you die.'

She laughed. Biff said I was only half-sharp. Janey laughed at me too and I felt hurt and ashamed at what I had said. But the girl laughed again, longer this time, the sound almost happy, and then suddenly she ruffled her hand in my hair and said:

'You'll do. You're all right. You keep me laughing, won't you?'

A few moments later we crossed the stream. It was only two or three inches deep there and full of flat white stones. There were always sticklebacks there and minnows that came darting out from under the shadow of the stones and I remembered how once we had caught crayfish under a stone and didn't know what it was.

The first to go through the stream was Bonzo and then after him the girl. She went over with the same long springing strides as she had used all the way up through the fields and now she seemed completely unaware of the stones. She went straight through the water up to her ankles, slopping forward, her shoes oozing water as she climbed the bank on the other side.

'How much farther?' She turned and almost shouted at us, as if we were still some distance behind.

'You got your feet all wet,' I said. 'Look at your shoes –'

She didn't look at her shoes. Instead she looked up at

the sky and I saw the sun shine flat into her large dark eyes with their heavy under-bruises, and in the steely forks of the pins that she still hadn't fixed properly into her hair.

'How much farther now?' she said. 'Is it far?'

'You can almost see it now,' Biff said. 'You'll see it when we get to the top of the field.'

At the crest of the slope that went up from that side of the stream ran a line of hawthorn trees with cow-worn trunks, where that afternoon sheep were lying, panting in the shade. These trees cut off, until you got near enough to see through them, the view over the fields towards the bullock-yard, the stable and the barn.

She reached the trees, with Bonzo, half a minute before us. She didn't seem to see the sheep, any more than she had seen the stones in the brook. She simply went blundering under the trees without stopping, making the sheep stumble up on their knees and then herd away together, bunting and alarmed, disturbed by the dog, into deeper shade.

After that we didn't try to catch her. By the time we got to the bullock-yard she had disappeared through the door of the stable, which was open now.

All I could see was the white shape of Bonzo, squatting on the threshold, a white splash that looked no bigger than a bird-dropping in the black covering shadow of the sycamore.

If it had seemed an hour or so while we waited by the pond for the man with the gun to move away it seemed like a whole afternoon while we waited, sitting on the gate of the bullock-yard, for someone to come out of the stable and into the yard.

Once I thought of the man being dead from drinking water. I even thought I wanted him to be dead. Then Biff and Janey would know that I was right and wouldn't laugh at me any more.

'I think he's died,' I said. 'I think he's dead from the water.'

'Oh! What the pipe,' Biff said. 'Everybody's always dead with you. You always imagine things. Sit still. You'll make me drop my glasses. We shan't bring him next time, shall we, Janey? It'll be just me and you next time, won't it, Janey?'

'I think he's dead too,' she said. 'If he's not, why is she so long in there?'

After that Biff didn't say so much. He went on huffily polishing his glasses over and over again, taking them off and then squinting through them and putting them back on his nose again.

Suddenly I knew that Janey was frightened. She jumped down from the gate and started to walk away.

'Let's hide,' she said. 'I don't want to see any dead people. They have their eyes open and they never shut them.'

That was too much for me too. I knew the man must be dead now. I jumped down from the gate too, and then Biff jumped down. Then we all looked through the bars of the gate but there was still nothing to be seen outside the stable but the white shape of Bonzo in the open stable door, in the great dark shade of the sycamore.

'Where shall we hide?' I said.

We ran some distance along the cart-track. Then we hid behind a bush of elderberry. We sat there for a long time without speaking, smelling the rank deep odour of elderberry stems, waiting for something to happen, and then Janey, who was always so quick, said:

'I heard the gate click. Didn't you hear?'

A minute or so later the man and the girl walked past us, down the track. I noticed the girl had washed the blood from her arms and had combed and pinned her hair. Only a second or two later Bonzo came after them, ten or fifteen feet behind. The man was carrying the black oil-cloth bag now and the dog seemed to fix his eyes on it, his nose close to the ground. With his other hand the man had taken the girl by the shoulders, and his hand kept moving across her shoulder, smoothing it down.

'Bonzo,' we whispered. 'Here. Good Bonzo. Here, Bonz, old boy – here.'

He went straight past us without looking at the elderberry tree. His eyes were simply fixed on the feet of the man, the wet shoes of the girl and the oil-cloth bag. We whispered after him once or twice again but he took no notice. The last we saw of him was when he squirmed through the gap of the hedge and turned, following the girl and the man down the road.

'Come on,' Biff said. 'Let's see where they go.'

Twenty minutes later we were standing on the high iron railway bridge that spanned the single-track line at the little branch station on that side of the town. We had to wait about ten minutes for the signals to change for the train. During all that time the man and the girl, with

Bonzo, stood on the platform, below us and about thirty yards away.

I noticed they didn't talk much. Sometimes the man looked up and down the track in the evening sunshine. His face, I thought, didn't look so old any longer. It didn't look so grey and prickled and drawn as before. He even smiled once or twice. And once I saw the girl stare quickly down at the platform, biting her lips, rather as if she couldn't bear it if he smiled.

Then the train came in, making clouds of smoke, as it went under the bridge where we were looking through the ironwork. By the time the smoke had begun to clear away the train had stopped in the station, doors were opening and shutting, and in another moment or two the man and the girl were in the train.

For a moment or two Bonzo was alone on the platform. Then Biff put his fingers into his mouth and gave a quick sharp whistle and the dog looked up. It seemed, for a second or two, as if he had heard us and knew we were there. Then there was another whistle, this time from the guard of the train, and in another second the dog jumped into the train.

'Good old Bonz,' Biff said. The train began to draw out of the station, its smoke dark yellow against the sun. 'So long, Bonz.'

'So long, Bonz,' I said.

'So long, Bonz,' Janey said. 'Goodbye.'

That night it was still light when I went to bed. It was hot in the bedroom and I was still excited. But I was not so excited about Bonzo, the man with the gun, and what a great and wonderful day it had been as about another thing.

'You said you could die,' I told my father, 'if you drank water out of a barrel. But there was a man today, he had a dog named Bonzo and he drank water with worms in it and he didn't die.'

'Go to sleep now,' my father said. 'Never mind about that. I said you would die *after it*. That's all. Go to sleep now.'

But I couldn't sleep. For a long time I lay awake, staring at the summer sky as it darkened, pale yellow to orange and then to the dusky colour of the smoke from the train. After the long day I was tired but not sleepy and I wasn't frightened any more. Now I knew that you didn't always die when you thought you would and that often, after all, there was no need to be afraid.

I began to think instead about the martin's eggs. We had four eggs. Biff had two, Janey one, and I had the other. In the morning I would make two pin-holes in my egg, blow it into a cup and then hang it in my bedroom on a string.

The Butterfly

MR PASCOE, laughing, made himself another piece of toast. It popped from the automatic toaster like a wingless dying bird shot by an invisible gun, laying itself on the appliqué tablecloth with the neatness of a brown plucked offering. Mr Pascoe spread butter on it with pleasant smoothing strokes and said:

'Is there anything you want? Something you feel you'd like to have?'

Outside, in the garden, heat was already beginning to quiver beyond a low line of rambler roses, burning in tremulous waves that reminded the boy of the air that danced above the hot bellies of steam rollers on tarry streets in summertime. To his father the toaster was a plaything he used every breakfast time.

'No. I don't think so,' he said.

'Now is the time to say if there is.'

'I don't think so.'

'What about a bow and arrow? You were keen on that last time.'

'I don't think so.' The boy saw the summer heat above the rambler roses crinkle as if from a fire. 'I think it's going to be too hot –'

'Hot?' his father said. 'I don't think you have the slightest idea what hot is.'

Another piece of toast leapt like a dying bird from the toaster. Mr Pascoe made an attempt to catch it, one-handed, with what was to have been amusing brilliance, but failed. He laughed, revealing brown crumbs of toast on his bluish lips. The toaster was very funny; he did not know quite why the toaster always made him laugh so much and yet failed to amuse the boy.

'We have a hundred and thirty degrees sometimes,' he said. 'You feel your eye-balls frizzle.'

'You said you would bring me a butterfly,' the boy said. 'One of the big blue ones.'

'I did?' Mr Pascoe found it hard to remember when he had made promises about a butterfly. 'I can't remember that.'

'It was when you and Mother went to Kwala Pilah with Mr Kitson —'

'Oh! that fellow.'

He destroyed the second piece of toast with a snap of his fingers, breaking it into singed fragments which he began to pick up with the buttery end of his knife.

'Well, is there anything you want? Have you thought of anything?'

'Only the butterfly.'

'No: I mean here. Before I go. There's only this morning. You could go into town with Miss Jackson. Or both of you could come with me.'

As the boy stared at the hot rambler roses, thinking first of Miss Jackson, who had wet slobbery teeth like a dog, and then of his father and mother going with Mr Kitson for the drive on which they had seen the butterflies, he could not understand why his father did not remember that trip. His mother remembered it perfectly.

'So large — as large as my hands.' He recalled with acute

vividness the fanning spread of his mother's delicate fingers as she vivaciously described for him the great width of the butterflies. 'It was at the top of that hill. They came out of the tree ferns – because don't you remember John Kitson said he thought for a moment they were blue hibiscus?'

His mother's fingers were a lovely pale yellow, with grey-pink nails, but when he remembered her it was easy to think of them as a brilliant scorching blue, dancing and unfolding like wings.

That was two years ago, but he remembered it perfectly. 'We should bring Peter one next time we come home,' his mother said, and his father said: 'Oh! you know how it is. Things get smashed up. You want the thing properly mounted –'

'Well, all right. We can get it properly mounted. There's no need to snap about it –'

'Oh! all right, we'll get it mounted then. There's a fellow in the Palmerston Road.'

'You will love it,' his mother said. 'I shall never forget seeing them on that hill. Marvellous. Crowds of them flying off like petals. As blue as cornflowers.'

'Switch off the toaster,' his father said. 'We don't want it any more.'

He had an idea his father had bought the toaster to amuse him because his mother had not come back. He supposed that was why he laughed so much every time the toast jumped out. 'We had one exactly like it in Singapore. They're American. I didn't think you could get them here.'

Miss Jackson had a habit of snapping her wet teeth

down over her bottom lip whenever he spoke of his mother. Miss Jackson didn't know why his mother hadn't come back; she had a good reason no doubt, a perfectly good reason; it was no use asking her. His father said: 'You've got to remember the trip is very expensive for two people. We had an idea I could come this year and then your mother could come next. That will save you that big gap.'

In winter, on the coldest, darkest days, he was obsessed with a feeling that summer would never come. His father and mother always came home in the summer so as to escape the worst of the equatorial weather. He had to wait a long time for the summer. His mother was beautifully thin and nervous and excitable and in summer she wore white silk dresses made by a Chinese dressmaker and the silk made her look more sheer, more exquisite and more lively than ever.

His mother liked joking too; but not in the way his father liked joking. He could not always laugh at the things his father thought were funny, but his mother was mischievous and her sort of laughter was catching.

He remembered running with her in the garden, in full summer, when the currant-trees were thick. His father began calling her and she said: 'Hide, lie down. Let's hide so he can't find us any more,' and he remembered how they lay behind the currant-trees, on hot earth, in secret, laughing all the time his father called. 'He can't find us! – he'll never find us again!' she said and he hid his face in her cool silky dress and smelled her body and the scent of silk and strong currant leaves and hot earth. That was the funniest thing they had ever done together.

His father did not think it funny. The boy remembered a darkness in his face. 'Oh! of course if you think it funny that's perfectly all right. That's all there is to it of course.'

It was not exactly anger his father felt. The hairs of his face seemed to bristle pompously. That was funny too and after he had stalked into the house the boy and his mother began laughing again, pressing their faces into their hands. He thought his mother would never stop laughing, but at last she said:

'Now we've really got to stop. We must. Peter, we mustn't laugh at people.' Bubbles of laughter kept bursting through her handkerchief as she dried her eyes. Tears of laughter made her eyes more lively and more beautiful. 'Now we've really got to stop – Peter, we really must – Oh! good Lord, I'm going to start again –!'

He knew that day that he belonged to his mother. All his feelings for her were enshrined in the laughter, the smell of hot currant leaves and hot earth, the secretive feeling of the white silk dress.

When she went away again Miss Jackson took charge of him. He could not see that there was really any reason for the existence of Miss Jackson, but his father explained that:

'We must keep the house on. You must have somewhere you can think of as home.'

In winter the currant-trees were bare, with big fat buds on them. Snow came and the feeling of summer became for ever destroyed. Miss Jackson hung pieces of bread and bacon-rind in apple-boughs above the lawn in frosty weather and blue-tits swung on the brown bristly skin and punctured the fat until it was knobbly like the paper he found in chocolate boxes. He watched the blue-tits and wondered if they were as blue as the butterflies of which his mother talked. He thought the butterflies must be even bigger, bluer and more wonderful. With her vivacious spreading hands his mother had made them seem like that.

'I am going to get a hair-cut,' his father said. 'You could come down in the car with me and then if there was anything you wanted –'

'Would you see if you can think of the butterfly next time?' the boy said. He knew that his mother would not fail to remember it and he said:

'Tie a piece of cotton round your finger. That's what Miss Jackson does. Then you'll remember it was the time you and Mummy went on the drive with Mr Kitson –'

'What makes you keep talking about Kitson?' his father said. 'Who spoke to you about Kitson?'

'Mother did. She used to talk about him –'

'What sort of talk? In what way?'

'I can't remember,' he said. 'It was just –'

'Did she talk often? Can't you remember if she talked often?'

'No. Just sometimes. Only just laughing and talking sometimes.'

His father's face was cloudy and stodgy. He searched it vainly for a break of light, a touch of the vivacity he found in his mother's, even a remnant of the breakfast humour about the toaster. All of his father seemed instead to recede, to stiffen and dry up. He got up from the table and said:

'Perhaps after all it would be better if you stayed in the garden. You could help Miss Jackson shell peas or something.'

The boy stared from the window at the hot quivering rambler roses. His father seemed as if he suddenly saw in his face a reflection of his own stodgy gravity and he said:

'Now you're not going to mope, are you? Just because I spoke. You said you wouldn't do that.'

'No.' He knew his father was angry because he had spoken of Mr Kitson.

'You're getting too big for that. You're nearly seven. And I've got something to tell you –' He paused and then manufactured, with a quick spurt of the lips, a sudden smile. 'I've been saving this up for you.'

'Yes?'

'On your birthday,' Mr Pascoe said, 'I'm going to ring you up. I'm going to telephone all the way from the Straits and say Hullo and wish you many happy returns.'

'I see.'

'I had the idea on the plane. I thought how wonderful it would be.'

'Shall I be able to talk to both of you?'

'It's nearly ten thousand miles,' Mr Pascoe said. 'But if we're lucky you'll be able to hear me just as clear as now. Only when I'm speaking it won't be exactly the same time as it is with you.'

'Why won't it?'

'It never is. It's to do with the earth going round.'

'Shall I be able to talk to both of you?'

'You can talk as long as you like,' Mr Pascoe said. 'Six minutes if you like. It's expensive but it doesn't matter.'

'What about Mother? Will she be there –?'

'Yes, yes. I said so, didn't I? We'll arrange all that.'

He tried to imagine the voice of his mother and father talking to him across the world. It seemed strange; it did not excite him very much; and he felt he would rather have had the butterfly. Since his mother had not come back there were times when his head seemed to grow large and hollow and droning with the sound of his own blood wandering through it; and soon it was his whole self, wandering about the world. His head and the world: droning and empty and hollow and echoing, and himself striding with rubbery steps across it, all alone, bouncing. It was the lightheadedness, Miss Jackson said. A powder would put that right. It was the dreams again, after too much supper. It was head under the clothes again. That was no good, this hot weather, that was a habit he must get out of.

'Well, I'll go now and have my wool shorn,' his father said. 'Are you sure there's nothing you want?'

'No, thank you.'

'Now's the time to say. It'll be too late tomorrow.'

'No, thank you.'

After his father had gone he went into the garden and stood there alone, watching the quiver of heat above the rambler roses. The leaves on the apple trees were very thick, hiding the dirty pieces of string on which Miss Jackson hung ham-rind in the winter. He thought of the day when he and his mother had hidden behind the currant-trees and she had said 'Let's hide so that he can't find us any more.' His birthday was a long way away, in December. He tried to imagine what it would be like in winter, with the birds pecking at ham-rind on frosty boughs, with dark afternoons and windy rain and the voice of his mother coming to meet him across the world.

When his father came back from having the hair-cut he must remember to tell him about the string on his finger, so that he in turn would remember to tell his mother about the butterfly and the wonderful day with Mr Kitson in the hills.

He remembered his mother's hands, fanning and excitable and wing-like, so that she too was like a butterfly. With the string on his finger his father would surely remember them too?

Love in a Wych Elm

WHEN I was a boy the Candleton sisters, seven of them, lived in a large gabled house built of red brick that gave the impression of having been muted by continual sunlight to a pleasant shade of orange-rose. The front face of it had a high, benign open appearance and I always felt that the big sash windows actually smiled down on the long gravel terrace, the iron pergola of roses and the sunken tennis lawn. At the back were rows of stables, all in the same faded and agreeable shade of brick, with lofts above them that were full of insecure and ancient bedsteads, fire-guards, hip-baths, tennis rackets, croquet hammers, rocking horses, muscle-developers, Indian clubs, travelling trunks and things of that sort thrown out by Mr and Mrs Candleton over the course of their fruitful years.

I was never very sure of what Mr Candleton did in life; I was not even sure in fact if he did anything at all except to induce Mrs Candleton, at very regular intervals, to bear another daughter. In a town like Evensford there were at that time very few people of independent means who lived in houses that had stables at the back. The Candletons were, or so it seemed to me, above our station. There was at one time a story that Mr Candleton was connected with wine. I could well believe this. Like his house, Mr Candleton's face had toned to a remarkably pleasant shade of inflammable rose. This always seemed perhaps brighter than it really was because his eyes were so blue. They were of that rare shade of pale violet blue that always seems about to dissolve, especially in intoxication. This effect was still further heightened by hair of a most pure distinguished shade of yellow: a thick oat-straw yellow that was quite startling and remarkable in a male.

All the Candleton sisters too had their father's pale violet dissolving eyes and that exceptional shade of oat-straw hair.

At first, when they were very small children, it was white and silky. Then as they grew up its characteristic shining straw-colour grew stronger. A stranger seeing them for the first time would have said that they were seven dolls who had been dipped in a solution of something several shades paler than saffron. The hair was very beautiful when brushed and as children they all wore it long.

On hot days in summer Mr Candleton wore cream flannel trousers with a blue pin stripe in them, a blazer with red and orange stripes, and a straw hat with a band of the same design. Round his waist he wore a red silk cummerbund. All his shirts were of silk and he always wore them buttoned at the neck. In winter he wore things like Donegal tweeds: roughish, sporting, oatmeal affairs that were just right for his grained waterproof shooting brogues. He wore smart yellow gloves and a soft tweed hat with a little feather in the band. He always seemed to be setting off somewhere, brisk and dandyish and correct, a man of leisure with plenty of time to spare.

It was quite different with Mrs Candleton. The house was big and rambling and it might well have been built

specially to accommodate Mrs Candleton, who was like a
big, absent-minded, untidy, roving bear. My mother used
to say that she got up and went to bed in a pinafore. It
wasn't a very clean pinafore either. Nor were her paper
hair-curlers, which were sometimes still in her rough un-
ruly black hair at tea-time. She always seemed to be wearing carpet-slippers and sometimes her stockings would be
slipping down. She was a woman who always seemed to
be catching up with life and was always a day and a half
behind.

The fact was, I suppose, that with seven children in
something like a dozen years Mrs Candleton was still
naturally hazy in some of her diurnal calculations. Instead of her catching up with life, life was always catching
up with her.

Meals, for example, made the oddest appearances in the
Candleton household. If I went on a school-less day to
call on Stella – she was the one exactly of my own age, the
one I knew best – it was either to find breakfast being
taken at eleven-thirty, with Mr Candleton always im-
maculate behind the silver toast-rack and Mrs Candleton
looking like the jaded mistress of a rag-and-bone man, or
dinner at half-past three or tea at seven. In a town like
Evensford everybody was rigidly governed by factory
hours and the sound of factory hooters. At various times
of the day silences fell on the town that were a hushed in-
dication that all honest people were decently at work. All
this meant that breakfast was at seven, dinner at twelve-
thirty and tea at half past five. That was how everybody
ate and lived and ran their lives in Evensford: everybody,
that is, except the Candletons.

These characteristics of excessive and immediate smartness on the one hand and the hair-curler and pinafore style on the other had been bequeathed by her and Mr Candleton in almost exactly equal measure to their children. The girls were all beautiful, all excessively dressy as they grew up and, as my mother was fond of saying, not over clean.

'If they get a cat-lick once a week it's about as much as they do get,' was one of her favourite sayings.

But children do not notice such things very acutely and I cannot say that I myself was very interested in the virtues of soap and water. What I liked about the Candletons was not only a certain mysterious quality of what I thought was aristocracy but a feeling of untamed irresponsibility. They were effervescent. When the eldest girl, Lorna, was seventeen she ran off with a Captain in the Royal Artillery who turned out to be a married man. I thought it might well have been the sort of thing that would have ruined a girl, temporarily at least, in Evensford, but Stella simply thought it a wild joke and said:

'She had a wonderful time. It was gorgeous. They stayed at a marvellous hotel in London. She told us all about it. I thought Mother would die laughing.'

Of laughing, not shame; that was typical of the Candleton standard, the Candleton approach and the Candleton judgement on such things.

The four eldest girls, two of them twins, were called Lorna, Hilda, Rosa and Freda. This habit of giving names ending in the same letter went on to Stella, with whom I played street-games in winter in front of the gas-lit windows of a pork-pie and sausage shop and games in summer in the Candleton garden and among the muscle-developers and bedsteads of the Candleton loft, and then on to the two youngest, who were mere babies as I knew them, Wanda and Eva. Mrs Candleton's Christian name was Blanche, which suited her perfectly.

It was a common tendency in all the Candleton girls to develop swiftly. At thirteen they were filling out; at fifteen they were splendidly and handsomely buxom and were doing up their hair. Hilda appeared to me to be a goddess of marbled form long before she was eighteen and got engaged to a beefy young farmer who bred prize cattle and called for her in a long open sports car.

Hilda had another characteristic not shared by any of the rest of the family except her mother. She sang rather well. At eighteen she began to have her pleasant, throaty, contralto voice trained. Mr Candleton was a strict Sunday morning churchgoer in pin-stripe trousers, bowler hat and spats, and Hilda went with him to sing in the choir. Her voice was trained by a Mr Lancaster, a rather bumptious pint-size tenor who gave her lessons three evenings a week. It was generally known that Mr Lancaster was, as a singer at any rate, past his best, but it was not long before the engagement between Hilda and the farmer was broken.

At that time Stella and I were nine. I, at least, was nine and Stella, physically, was twelve or thirteen. What I liked about her so much in those days was her utter freedom to come and go as she pleased. Other children had errands to run, confirmation classes to attend, catechisms to learn, aunts to visit, restrictive penances like shoes to clean or knives to rub up with bath-brick.

In the Candleton way she had never anything to do but play, enjoy herself, indulge in inconsequential make-believe and teach me remarkable things about life and living.

'What shall we do? Let's be married. Let's go up to the loft and be married.'

'We were married the day before yesterday.'

'That doesn't matter. You can be married over and over again. Hilda's going to be. Come on, let's be married.'

'All right. But not in the loft. Let's have a new house this time.'

'All right. Let's be married in the wych-elm.'

The Candleton garden extended beyond the stables into a rough orchard of old damson trees, with a few crooked espalier pears. A pepper-pot summer house in rustic work with a thatched roof stood in one corner, almost obliterated by lilac trees. In summer damsons and pears fell into the deep grass and no one picked them up. A sense of honeyed rotting quietness spread under the lurching trees and was compressed and shut in by a high boundary line of old, tapering wych-elms.

Rooks nested in the highest of the elms and when summer thickened the branches the trees were like a wall. The house was hidden and shut away. On a heavy summer day you would hear nothing there but the sound of rooks musing and croaking and fruit falling with a squashy mellow plop on the grass and paths.

Up in the wych-elms the peculiar structure of boughs made a house for us. We could walk about it. We crawled like monkeys, from tree to tree. In this paradise we stayed for entire afternoons, cocooned with scents, hidden away in leaves. We made tea in ancient saucepans on flameless fires of elm twigs and prepared dinners of potatoes and gravy from fallen pears. And up here, on a soft August afternoon, we were married without witnesses and Stella, with her yellow hair done up for the first time, wore a veil of lace curtains and carried a bunch of cow-parsley.

But before that happened I had caught, only the day before, another glimpse of the Candleton way of living.

I had called about six o'clock in the evening for Stella but although the door of the house was open nobody, for some time at any rate, answered my ring at the bell. That was not at all unusual at the Candleton household. Although it never seemed possible for nine such unmistakable people to disappear without trace it was frequently happening and often I went to the door and rang until I was tired of ringing and then went away without an answer.

I remember once ringing the bell and then, tired of it, peeping into the kitchen. It was one of those big old-fashioned kitchens with an enormous iron cooking range with plate racks above it and gigantic dressers and vast fish-kettles and knife-cleaners everywhere. In the middle of it all Mrs Candleton sat asleep. Not normally asleep, I could see. A quarter-full bottle of something for which I had no definition stood on the table in front of her, together with a glass and, beside the glass, most astonishing thing of all, her false teeth.

Blowsily, frowsily, comfortably, toothlessly, Mrs Candleton was sleeping away the afternoon in her hair-curlers and her pinafore.

But on the evening I called for Stella the kitchen was empty. I rang the bell four or five times and then, getting no answer, stepped into the hall.

'Hullo,' someone said.

That very soft, whispered throaty voice was Hilda's. She was standing at the top of the stairs. She was wearing nothing but her petticoat and her feet were bare. In her hands she was holding a pair of stockings, which she had evidently been turning inside out in readiness to put on.

'Oh! it's you,' she said. 'I thought I heard someone.'

'Is Stella here?'

'They're all out. They've all gone to the Robinsons' for tea. It's Katie's birthday.'

'Oh! I see,' I said. 'Well, I'll come again tomorrow –'

'I'm just going to a dance,' she said. 'Would you like to see my dress? Would you? – come on, come up.'

Standing in the bedroom, with the August sunlight shining on her bare shoulders, through the lace of her slip and on her sensational yellow Candleton hair, she was a magnificent figure of a girl.

'Just let me put my stockings on and then you can see my dress.'

She sat down on the bed to put on her stockings. Her legs were smooth and heavy. I experienced an odd sensation as the stockings unrolled up her legs and then were fastened somewhere underneath the petticoat. Then she stood up and looked at the back of her legs to see if her stockings were straight. After that she smoothed the straps of her petticoat over her shoulders and said:

'Just wait till I give my hair one more brush.'

I shall never forget how she sat before the dressing

mirror and brushed her hair. I was agreeably and mystically stunned. The strokes of the brush made her hair shine exactly, as I have said before, like oat-straw. Nothing could have been purer and more shining. It was marvellously burnished and she laughed at me in the mirror because I stood there so staring and speechless and stunned.

'Well, do I look nice? You think I shall pass in a crowd?'

'Yes.'

'That's good. It's nice to have a man's opinion.'

She laughed again and put on her dress. It was pure white, long and flouncy. I remember distinctly the square low collar. Then she put on her necklace. It was a single row of pearls and she couldn't fasten it.

'Here, you can do this,' she said.

She sat on the bed and I fastened the necklace. The young hair at the nape of her neck was like yellow chicken down. I was too confused to notice whether she had washed her neck or not and then she said:

'That's it. Now just a little of this and I'm ready.'

She sprayed her hair, her arms and the central shadow of her bosom with scent from a spray.

'How about a little for you?'

She sprayed my hair and in a final moment of insupportable intoxication I was lost in a wave of wallflowers.

'That's the most expensive scent there is,' she said. 'The most difficult to make. Wallflowers.'

Perhaps it was only natural, next day, as I came to be married to Stella high at the altar of the wych-elms, that I found myself oppressed by a sensation of anti-climax.

Something about Stella, I felt, had not quite ripened. I had not the remotest idea as to what it could be except that she seemed, in some unelevating and puzzling way, awkward and flat.

'What do you keep staring at me for?'

'I'm just going to spray you with scent,' I said. 'There – piff! pish! pfiff –'

'Whatever made you think of that?'

I was afraid to speak of Hilda and I said:

'All girls have to have scent on when they're married.'

'Do I look nice?'

She didn't really look nice. The lace curtain was mouldy in one corner and had holes down one side. I didn't like the odour of cow-parsley. But the soft golden oat-straw hair was as remarkable as ever and I said:

'You look all right.'

Then we were married. After we were married she said:

'Now you have to make love to me.'

'Why?'

'Everybody has to make love when they're married.'

I looked at her in utter mystification. Then suddenly she dropped the cow-parsley and pushed back her veil and kissed me. She held me in an obliterating and momentary bondage by the trunk of the wych-elm, kissing me with such blistering force that I lost my cap. I was rather upset about my cap as it fell in the nettles below but she said:

'Sit down. We're in bed now. We have to be in bed now we're married. It's the first thing people do.'

'Why?'

'Don't you know?'

I did not know; nor, as it happens, did she. But one of the advantages of being born one of a family of seven sisters is that you arrive much earlier at the approximation of the more delicate truths than you do if you are a boy. Perhaps in this respect I was a backward boy, but I could only think it was rather comfortless trying to make love in a wych-elm and after a time I said:

'Let's go and play in the loft now.'

'What with?'

'I don't know,' I said. 'Let's have a change. We've been married an awful lot of times –'

'I know,' she said. 'We'll play with the chest-developers.'

While we played in the loft with the chest-developers she had an original thought.

'I think if I practise a lot with these I shall get fat up top more quickly.'

'You will?'

'I think I shall soon anyway.'

Like Hilda, I thought. A renewed sensation of agreeable and stupefying delight, together with a scent of wall-flowers, shot deliciously through me and I was half-way to the realization of the truth that girls are pleasant things when she said:

'One day, when we're big, let's be really married, shall us?'

'All right.'

'Promise?'

'Yes,' I said.

'You know what you'll be when you're married to me, don't you?' she said.

I couldn't think.

'You'll be a viscount,' she said.

'What's a viscount?'

'It's the husband of a viscountess.'

'How shall I come to be that?'

'Because a viscountess is the daughter of a lord.'

'But,' I said, 'your father isn't a lord.'

'No,' she said, 'but his brother is. He lives in a castle in Bedfordshire. It has a hundred and forty rooms in it. We go there every summer. And when he dies my father will be a lord.'

'Is he going to die?'

'Soon.'

'Supposing your father dies before he does?'

'Oh! he won't,' she said. 'He's the youngest son. The oldest always die first.'

She went on to tell me many other interesting things about our life together. Everything in that life would be of silk, she said, like her father's shirts. Silk sheets on the bed, silk pillows, silk tablecloths, silk cushions. 'And I shall always wear silk drawers,' she said. 'Even on week-days.'

Altogether, it seemed, we should have a marvellous life together.

'And we shall drink port wine for supper,' she said. 'Like my father does. He always drinks port wine for supper.'

'Is it nice?'

'Yes,' she said. 'I'm allowed to have it sometimes. You'll like it. You can get drunk as often as you like then. Like my father does.'

'Does he get drunk?'

'Not as often as my mother does,' she said, 'but quite a lot.'

I suppose I was shocked.

'Oh! that's all right,' she said. 'Lords always get drunk. That's why people always say "drunk as a lord". That's the proper thing to do.'

Armed with the chest-developers, we spent an ecstatic afternoon. I was so filled with the golden snobbery of being a viscount that it was a cold and dusty sort of shock when she told me that anyway we couldn't be married for years and years, not until she was fatter, like Hilda was.

The recollection of Hilda, all burnished and magnificent and intoxicating and perfumed, inflamed and inspired me to greater efforts with the chest-developers.

'We must work harder,' I said.

I wanted so much to be a lord, to live in a castle, to drink port wine and to be married to someone with silk drawers that I was totally unprepared for the shock my mother gave me.

'The little fibber, the little story-teller, the little liar,' she said.

'But she said so,' I said. 'She told me.'

'I went to board school with Reggie Candleton,' she said. 'He was in my class. They came from Gas Street.'

Nothing in the world was worse than coming from Gas Street. You could not go lower than Gas Street. The end of the respectable world was Gas Street.

'It's she who had the money,' my mother said. 'Mrs Candleton. Her father was a brewer and Reggie Candleton worked there. He was always such a little dandy. Such a little masher. Always the one for cutting such a dash.'

I decided it was wiser to say nothing about the prospect of marrying, or about Stella's urgent efforts with the chest-developers, or the silk drawers.

'All top show,' my mother said. 'That's what it is. All fancy fol-di-dols on top and everything dropping into rags underneath. Every one of them with hair like a ten-guinea doll and a neck you could sow carrots in.'

I don't suppose for a moment that Stella remembers me; or that, on an uncomfortable, intimate occasion, we were married in a wych-elm. It is equally unlikely that Hilda remembers me; or that, with her incomparable yellow hair, her white dance dress, her soft blonde flesh and her rare scent of wallflowers, she once asked me to give her my opinion as a man. I believe Stella is married to a bus-conductor. The rest of the Candletons have faded from my life. With the summer frocks, the summer straw-hats and the summer flannels, the cummerbunds, the silk shirts, the elegant brogues, the chest-developers and the incomparable yellow hair they have joined Mr Candleton in misty, muted, permanent bankruptcy.

Love in a wych-elm is not an easy thing; but like the Candletons it is unforgettable.

The House with the Grape Vine

WHEN he was a small boy he lived in a street that plunged down a long steep hill between lines of hard-baked bricks that were more like boxes than houses, and here and there a factory that was like a taller darker box with the iron limb of a crane hanging like a gallows outside.

There were no trees in that street. But once, his father would tell him, and not so long ago, it had been a place of green fields, with oats and barley and meadows where there were now factory yards, and little spinneys of violets and a farmhouse with apple-trees and a brook at the foot of the hill where sticklebacks swam among the cresses.

'And the farmhouse,' his father would say, 'had a grape-vine. Like all the other old houses in the town. Nearly every one of them, in those days, had a grape-vine.'

'With grapes on?'

'Of course. Nice ones.'

'Green ones? Like the ones we have at Christmas?'

No, his father would tell him, they were black ones. Or rather, dark plum-coloured ones. Not big, of course, like those you bought in shops. 'But about as big as your marbles,' he would say.

'And whereabouts on the farmhouse did the grape-vine grow?'

'On the south side. The other side from the road. It went all along that wall of the house. You couldn't see it from the road.'

'Then how did you know it was there?'

'Because,' his father would tell him, 'I used to work there.'

That was a very wonderful thing, he thought, the fact that his father had worked at a farmhouse.

'I never knew that,' he said. 'Did you work there all the time?'

'No,' his father said. 'Not all the time. Half-time.'

That was a thing he did not quite understand: half-time. But his father could explain that.

'In those days,' he said, 'we went to school half-time. School in the mornings and then work in the afternoons.'

That, too, he thought, was wonderful. Wasn't it fun, he said, only to have to go to school half the time and then work in the farmhouse for the rest of the time?

'No,' his father said, 'I hated it.'

That was something that was quite beyond him. He wished often that it would happen to him that he could go to school half the time and work among the apple-trees and the grape-vine for the rest of the time. That was the kind of life, he used to think, until his father said:

'I was eight. It was one winter when I worked there. There were no houses then between here and Evensford Hill in those days. I used to run all the way home in the dark, late at night, and my grandmother would be crying because she didn't know where I was.'

'Which granny was that?'

'She's dead now,' his father would tell him. 'My mother died first. And then my grandmother. And after that –'

And gradually he knew that his father had been alone after that: though exactly how much alone and how often alone he did not know until long afterwards. What he really cared about and what he really wanted to know about in those days was the farmhouse and the grape-vine and how the grapes grew and what it was like before the brick boxes and the factories with the gallows-cranes came to smother and obliterate it all.

'Do you think the grape-vine is still there?' he said.

'Well,' his father said, 'the house is still there. That's the only house left in the street. Of course the orchard isn't there. That was cut down when they built Packington's factory. But the old gates are there. And you can see it was a farm because it still has the stables there, and the pigeon-cote in the top.'

How marvellous it must have been, he thought, to have stables and a pigeon-cote in the yard instead of only a water-barrel and a slat fence where people beat their mats. What days they must have been – he simply couldn't believe his father hadn't liked them.

'Did you ever eat the grapes?'

'No.'

'Weren't they good to eat?'

'Oh! yes. Only it was winter-time when I was there.'

'But if you'd stayed till summer-time would you have had some to eat?'

'There was never a boy,' his father said, 'who asked so many questions.'

But every day, after that, when he went down-hill to school, and again when he came back, he began to stop outside the gates that were now wedged between the gas-tarred wall of a house and the gaunt walls of a factory. He was aware of wanting to make a link with the past. All he could see of this link were the blocked-up holes of the dove-cote in the stable, the stone walls of the house and once, when he peered through the key-hole of the gate, a big dog-kennel with a dirty dinner-plate outside.

'When did the grapes ripen?' he said once.

'About September time.'

Then he had a final, uneasy, haunting question:

'Weren't you very happy there?'

'No.'

'Why not?'

'It isn't worth going into. It isn't worth bothering your head about.'

'What did you have to do there? What work?'

'Oh! cleaning the hens out and cleaning the pigeons out. And sweeping the yard. And cleaning knives. And running errands. And looking for eggs – you know the sort of thing.'

Yes: he knew the sort of thing. And again he could not think, for the life of him, why his father hadn't liked it.

'I just didn't,' his father said. 'I can't explain why. Perhaps some day there will be something that will make you unhappy and you won't know why it is. I hope not. But you can't always explain things. Things are funny that way sometimes.'

Yes: things were funny, he thought. Grown-up people were funny too.

He supposed he must have waited for three months or more, all through summer and into September, before he had courage enough to jump up and flick down the latch of the old house gate and then go, for the first time, into the yard the other side.

He always remembered that day. It might have been chosen specially from all the days of the autumn because the air was so yellow with sunshine that the stone of the house seemed almost the colour of a piece of plain Madeira cake, and because even the small white clouds seemed warm.

To his surprise and joy there were also two or three apple-trees, and a single pear, in the little garden beyond the stables. In the yard an old dog lay asleep by the kennel like a flabby bag of mangy brown leather with irregular black patches on its sides.

He was very terrified of dogs and he went across the yard in a wide circuit, on tip-toe, looking backwards all the time over his shoulder.

And then all at once an old lady had him by the scruff of his collar. Her long hand pounced out from behind the corner of the house. With a cry she thrust into his eyes a long face like a parsnip that had a few suspended hairy roots hanging from the chin.

'Ah! you never see me, you never see me, did you?' she said. 'You never see me.'

It was impossible to speak; there was only a terrible thunder in all his veins.

'I know what you come for, I know what you come for. You come nickin' apples, didn't you, you come nickin' apples. Scrumpin' – nickin' other folkses things – scrumpin' – that's what you come for!'

He felt the horrible wiry hairs of her chin brush the back of his neck. He heard the dog stir on its chain and the sound came to him like the turn of a lock, imprisoning him there in the yard alone with her.

'That's what you come for, didn't you? I know. I catch 'em all the time. Every day. They're allus in here – but I git 'em. Like I got you –'

'I never –'

'Never what? If you didn't come for nickin' things what did you come for?'

There was a great cold stone in his throat. He swallowed several times but it wouldn't go down.

'Grapes,' he managed to say at last. 'That's all I came for. Somebody said you had grapes to sell –'

'Grapes? Grapes? Somebody? – who's somebody? Who says so?'

'They said you had a grape-vine – on the house. They said –'

'Grapes? They's never bin grapes here, not on this house, not since I lived here, and that's bin years a-new.'

And suddenly she lifted him with her long skinny arm clean off the ground, screeching into his face:

'You know what they do to little snots like you?'

All his life was streaming out in terror through the soles of his feet and he couldn't answer.

'They git the policeman. Tek you to police-station. Git you locked up there. Keep you in there so you can't nick things no more.'

Her eyes were so near to him and so distended and bright that he could see swimming flecks of blood in them. Then she gave a great suck of her lips, drawing breath through her teeth, and said:

'Grapes? Somebody said they was grapes, did they? Where?'

'On the house.'

'Come wi' me!' she screeched, 'and I'll jist show you whether they is!'

With her long bony arm she lugged him across the yard and round the corner of the house. He was so small that she could twirl him at the end of her arm like a rope.

'Well – there y'are! There's your grapes – there y'are!'

That was the wall of the house, he knew quite well, that his father had described. It faced away from the road. That was the wall all right, but there were no grapes on it. It was empty; there was nothing there.

'You're a fibber, ain't you? You're a story-teller, ain't you?' she said. 'You made it up, didn't you? You knew they wasn't no grapes there, didn't you? All the time. You tell lies.'

He knew there had been grapes there. He knew because his father had told him so; but he couldn't say anything and she screeched:

'You know what they do to little monkeys what tell lies? You know what I've a good mind to do to you?' With craggy fingers she pointed to the windows of the stable. 'Lock y'in there. Lock y'up in there while I git a policeman.'

'No,' he said. 'No –'

'I locked one in there once. All day. That was a lesson to him. He never came back, nickin' folkses things. Nickin' things that never belonged to him. Shall I lock y'in there? Shall I? –'

'No!' he screamed.

Then he broke from her and he was running. The dog began lashing to and fro on the chain. The old woman gave a wild double stamping scurry with her feet as if she were chasing him. He was too small to reach the latch of the gate and the first time he leapt for it he missed it.

'You come in here once more and I'll lock y'up,' she yelled, 'and git the policeman and git you put in jail,' and then he hit the latch and it was down and he was running in the street outside.

He never once spoke to his father about the grapes or the grape-vine after that. He did not ask another single question about the house, the winter his father worked there, the way he had run home late at night to a weeping grandmother, or why he had been unhappy.

It was not because he did not believe in the grape-vine; or that he believed his father had told a lie or had invented it or had made some mistake of memory about it over the years. He had great faith in his father. He knew that his father would not tell him a thing that was not right. He knew that his father would never let him be taken to the police-station, that awful place. His father would protect him. He trusted his father. His father was a wonderful, kindly man.

'But,' as his father said, 'things are funny that way sometimes. You can't explain them. Perhaps some day there will be something that will make you unhappy and you won't be able to explain it to anyone – not even to somebody you love.'

That was why, for ever afterwards, when he passed the gates of that house, he remembered the grape-vine. That was why he too hated that house and, because of it, loved his father so much more.

Great Uncle Crow

ONCE in the summer-time, when the water-lilies were in bloom and the wheat was new in ear, his grandfather took him on a long walk up the river, to see his Uncle Crow. He had heard so much of Uncle Crow, so much that was wonderful and to be marvelled at, and for such a long time, that he knew him to be, even before that, the most remarkable fisherman in the world.

'Masterpiece of a man, your Uncle Crow,' his grandfather said. 'He could git a clothes-line any day and tie a brick on it and a mossel of cake and go out and catch a pike as long as your arm.'

When he asked what kind of cake his grandfather seemed irritated and said it was just like a boy to ask questions of that sort.

'Any kind o' cake,' he said. 'Plum cake. Does it matter? Carraway cake. Christmas cake if you like. Anything. I shouldn't wonder if he could catch a pretty fair pike with a cold baked tater.'

'Only a pike?'

'Times,' his grandfather said, 'I've seen him sittin' on the bank on a sweltering hot day like a furnace, when nobody was gettin' a bite not even off a blood-sucker. And there your Uncle Crow'd be a-pullin' 'em out by the dozen, like a man shellin' harvest beans.'

'And how does he come to be my Uncle Crow?' he said, 'if my mother hasn't got a brother? Nor my father.'

'Well,' his grandfather said, 'he's really your mother's own cousin, if everybody had their rights. But all on us call him Uncle Crow.'

'And where does he live?'

'You'll see,' his grandfather said. 'All by hisself. In a little titty bit of a house by the river.'

The little titty bit of a house, when he first saw it, surprised him very much. It was not at all unlike a black tarred boat that had either slipped down a slope and stuck there on its way to launching or one that had been washed up and left there in a flood. The roof of brown tiles had a warp in it and the sides were mostly built, he thought, of tarred beer-barrels.

The two windows with their tiny panes were about as large as chessboards and Uncle Crow had nailed underneath each of them a sill of sheet tin that was still a brilliant blue, each with the words 'Backache Pills' in white lettering on it, upside down.

On all sides of the house grew tall feathered reeds. They enveloped it like gigantic whispering corn. Some distance beyond the great reeds the river went past in a broad slow arc, on magnificent kingly currents, full of long white islands of water-lilies, as big as china breakfast cups, shining and yellow-hearted in the sun.

He thought, on the whole, that that place, the river with the water-lilies, the little titty bit of a house, and the great forest of reeds talking between soft brown beards, was the nicest he had ever seen.

'Anybody about?' his grandfather called. 'Crow! – anybody at home?'

The door of the house was partly open, but at first there was no answer. His grandfather pushed open the door still farther with his foot. The reeds whispered down by the river and were answered, in the house, by a sound like the creak of bed springs.

'Who is't?'

'It's me, Crow,' his grandfather called. 'Lukey. Brought the boy over to have a look at you.'

A big gangling red-faced man with rusty hair came to the door. His trousers were black and very tight. His eyes were a smeary vivid blue, the same colour as the stripes of his shirt, and his trousers were kept up by a leather belt with brass escutcheons on it, like those on horses' harness.

'Thought very like you'd be out a-pikin',' his grandfather said.

'Too hot. How's Lukey boy? Ain't seed y' lately, Lukey boy.'

His lips were thick and very pink and wet, like cow's lips. He made a wonderful erupting jolly sound somewhat between a belch and a laugh.

'Comin' in it a minute?'

In the one room of the house was an iron bed with an old red check horse-rug spread over it and a stone copper in one corner and a bare wooden table with dirty plates and cups and a tin kettle on it. Two osier baskets and a scythe stood in another corner.

Uncle Crow stretched himself full length on the bed as if he was very tired. He put his knees in the air. His belly was tight as a bladder of lard in his black trousers, which were mossy green on the knees and seat.

'How's the fishin'?' his grandfather said. 'I bin tellin' the boy –'

Uncle Crow belched deeply. From where the sun struck full on the tarred wall of the house there was a hot whiff of baking tar. But when Uncle Crow belched there was a smell like the smell of yeast in the air.

'It ain't bin all that much of a summer yit,' Uncle Crow said. 'Ain't had the rain.'

'Not like that summer you catched the big 'un down at Archer's Mill. I recollect you a-tellin' on me –'

'Too hot and dry by half,' Uncle Crow said. 'Gits in your gullet like chaff.'

'You recollect that summer?' his grandfather said. 'Nobody else a-fetching on 'em out only you –'

'Have a drop o' neck-oil,' Uncle Crow said.

The boy wondered what neck-oil was and presently, to his surprise, Uncle Crow and his grandfather were drinking it. It came out of a dark-green bottle and it was a clear bright amber, like cold tea, in the two glasses.

'The medder were yeller with 'em,' Uncle Crow said. 'Yeller as a guinea.'

He smacked his lips with a marvellously juicy, fruity sound. The boy's grandfather gazed at the neck-oil and said he thought it would be a corker if it was kept a year or two, but Uncle Crow said:

'Trouble is, Lukey boy, it's a terrible job to keep it. You start tastin' on it to see if it'll keep and then you taste on it again and you go on tastin' on it until they ain't a drop left as 'll keep.'

Uncle Crow laughed so much that the bed springs cackled underneath his bouncing trousers.

'Why is it called neck-oil?' the boy said.

'Boy,' Uncle Crow said, 'when you git older, when you git growed-up, you know what'll happen to your gullet?'

'No.'

'It'll git sort o' rusted up inside. Like a old gutter pipe. So's you can't swaller very easy. Rusty as old Harry it'll git. You know that, boy?'

'No.'

'Well, it will. I'm tellin' on y'. And you know what y' got to do then?'

'No.'

'Every now and then you gotta git a drop o' neck-oil down it. So's to ease it. A drop o' neck-oil every once in a while – that's what you gotta do to keep the rust out.'

The boy was still contemplating the curious prospect of his neck rusting up inside in later years when Uncle Crow said: 'Boy, you go outside and jis' round the corner you'll see a bucket. You bring handful o' cresses out on it. I'll bet you're hungry, ain't you?'

'A little bit.'

He found the watercresses in the bucket, cool in the shadow of the little house, and when he got back inside with them Uncle Crow said:

'Now you put the cresses on that there plate there and then put your nose inside that there basin and see what's inside. What is't, eh?'

'Eggs.'

'Ought to be fourteen on 'em. Four-apiece and two over. What sort are they, boy?'

'Moor-hens'.'

'You got a knowin' boy here, Lukey,' Uncle Crow said.

He dropped the scaly red lid of one eye like an old cockerel going to sleep. He took another drop of neck-oil and gave another fruity, juicy laugh as he heaved his body from the bed. 'A very knowin' boy.'

Presently he was carving slices of thick brown bread with a great horn-handled shut-knife and pasting each slice with summery golden butter. Now and then he took another drink of neck-oil and once he said:

'You get the salt pot, boy, and empty a bit out on that there saucer, so's we can all dip in.'

Uncle Crow slapped the last slice of bread on to the buttered pile and then said:

'Boy, you take that there jug there and go a step or two up the path and dip yourself a drop o' spring water. You'll see it. It comes out of a little bit of a wall, jist by a doddle-willer.'

When the boy got back with the jug of spring water Uncle Crow was opening another bottle of neck-oil and his grandfather was saying: 'God a-mussy man, goo steady. You'll have me agoin' one way and another –'

'Man alive,' Uncle Crow said, 'and what's wrong with that?'

Then the watercress, the salt, the moor-hens' eggs, the spring water, and the neck-oil were all ready. The moor-hens' eggs were hard-boiled. Uncle Crow lay on the bed and cracked them with his teeth, just like big brown nuts, and said he thought the watercress was just about as nice and tender as a young lady.

'I'm sorry we ain't got the gold plate out though. I had it out a-Sunday.' He closed his old cockerel-lidded eye again and licked his tongue backwards and forwards across his lips and dipped another peeled egg in salt. 'You know what I had for my dinner a-Sunday, boy?'

'No.'

'A pussy-cat on a gold plate. Roasted with broad-beans and new taters. Did you ever heerd talk of anybody eatin' a roasted pussy-cat, boy?'

'Yes.'

'You did?'

'Yes,' he said, 'that's a hare.'

'You got a very knowin' boy here, Lukey,' Uncle Crow said. 'A very knowin' boy.'

Then he screwed up a big dark-green bouquet of watercress and dipped it in salt until it was entirely frosted and then crammed it in one neat wholesale bite into his soft pink mouth.

'But not on a gold plate?' he said.

He had to admit that.

'No, not on a gold plate,' he said.

All that time he thought the fresh watercress, the moorhens' eggs, the brown bread-and-butter, and the spring water were the most delicious, wonderful things he had ever eaten in the world. He felt that only one thing was missing. It was that whenever his grandfather spoke of fishing Uncle Crow simply took another draught of neck-oil.

'When are you goin' to take us fishing?' he said.

'You et up that there egg,' Uncle Crow said. 'That's the last one. You et that there egg up and I'll tell you what.'

'What about gooin' as far as that big deep hole where the chub lay?' grandfather said. 'Up by the back-brook –'

'I'll tell you what, boy,' Uncle Crow said, 'you git your grandfather to bring you over September time, of a morning, afore the steam's off the winders. Mushroomin' time. You come over and we'll have a bit o' bacon and mushroom for breakfast and then set into the pike. You see, boy, it ain't the pikin' season now. It's too hot. Too bright. It's too bright of afternoon, and they ain't a-bitin'.'

He took a long rich swig of neck-oil.

'Ain't that it, Lukey? That's the time, ain't it, mushroom time?'

'Thass it,' his grandfather said.

'Tot out,' Uncle Crow said. 'Drink up. My throat's jist easin' orf a bit.'

He gave another wonderful belching laugh and told the boy to be sure to finish up the last of the watercress and the bread-and-butter. The little room was rich with the smell of neck-oil, and the tarry sun-baked odour of the beer-barrels that formed its walls. And through the door came, always, the sound of reeds talking in their beards, and the scent of summer meadows drifting in from beyond the great curl of the river with its kingly currents and its islands of full blown lilies, white and yellow in the sun.

'I see the wheat's in ear,' his grandfather said. 'Ain't that the time for tench, when the wheat's in ear?'

'Mushroom time,' Uncle Crow said. 'That's the time. You git mushroom time here, and I'll fetch you a tench out as big as a cricket bat.'

He fixed the boy with an eye of wonderful, watery, glassy blue and licked his lips with a lazy tongue, and said:

'You know what colour a tench is, boy?'

'Yes,' he said.

'What colour?'

'The colour of the neck-oil.'

'Lukey,' Uncle Crow said, 'you got a very knowin' boy here. A very knowin' boy.'

After that, when there were no more cresses or moor-hens' eggs, or bread-and-butter to eat, and his grandfather said he'd get hung if he touched another drop of neck-oil, he and his grandfather walked home across the meadows.

'What work does Uncle Crow do?' he said.

'Uncle Crow? Work? – well, he ain't – Uncle Crow? Well, he works, but he ain't what you'd call a reg'lar worker –'

All the way home he could hear the reeds talking in their beards. He could see the water-lilies that reminded him so much of the gold and white inside the moor-hens' eggs. He could hear the happy sound of Uncle Crow laughing and sucking at the neck-oil, and crunching the fresh salty cresses into his mouth in the tarry little room.

He felt happy, too, and the sun was a gold plate in the sky.

Source of the World

THERE was a day when he went with Humph Mason up
the far reaches of the brook, beyond places he had never
seen before, almost, he fancied, into another country, to
find the source of the world.

That was what Humph Mason said it was called, and
Humph was his friend.

'Rivers go down into the sea,' Humph said. 'They've
got to. It's all downhill. But they come from somewhere.
Somewhere a long way away. A long way up, in mountains. That's called the source of the world.'

Humph wore big spectacles. They were so big and so
thick and so strong that he called them his bike lamps.
They magnified. Sometimes Humph let you wear them
for a few minutes. When he did you understood why the
world appeared so vastly different through Humph's eyes
from what it did through your own. It was like looking at
the world through two big glass marbles. Everything was
round and fat and pot-bellied and shining and wide:
rather like Humph himself was.

'We're men,' Humph said. 'We'll be gone days and
days. We'll have to go in marches.'

He had been to the brook, he supposed, at least about
a thousand times. There were eight fields he knew through
which it flowed: a little field covered with golden sheets
of dandelion in May, then a field where he had once found
a wild duck's nest among a clump of sloes, then the field

where you could drink from a spring that came from a
high bank and his grandfather said that was the purest,
clearest water in the world. Then a field he called the
watercress field, because the marshy places were dark with
cresses, and another he called the pussy-willow field, because the brook came down under golden arches of
flower at Easter-time. Then the crab-blossom field. Then
a field with a pool, under hawthorn-trees, that was something the shape of a long black harp, and where he had
seen the biggest fish of his life, a pike, lying like a dark
green sword on the top of the water.

And last of all the field where he used to cut arrows for
his bow: a field like a jungle, full of spears of reed waving
pale green ribbons of leaf in summer and shaggy feathers
of flower, like the head-dresses of African warriors, when
autumn came.

Beyond that he had never been. It could not be far beyond that, Humph said, before they found the source of
the world.

'Let's make camp,' Humph said, in the fourth of the
fields.

That was one of the fields he liked best. He loved it not
only because there was something friendly and good
about the marshy places dark with cresses but because, in
the brook itself, the water ran very bright and shallow
over stones as green as parsley and where sometimes, if
you were lucky, you could lie and watch schools of fish,
roach he thought they were, quivering and flickering
against the current in the sun.

They saw shoals of fish that day. At first he didn't think
they were very big fish, no bigger at any rate than he had

ever seen before. Then Humph said he could borrow his bike-lamps and when he put them on he saw that the fish were really as wide and flat as plaice, the fish his mother bought from the shop where smoky kippers hung on lines, looking just like shoes that had been run over by steam-rollers and varnished gold.

'By Golly,' Humph kept saying. 'By Golly. By Golly.'

His eyes looked funny without the spectacles: squeezed up and short-sighted and pale and not properly dressed somehow.

'We got to catch some,' Humph said. 'That'll be our food.'

'You have to tickle them underneath,' he said. 'That's how to get them.'

He lay on his belly, hanging over the bank. He could see the red fins of the fish winking in the dazzling water. Everything, through Humph's spectacles, was strange and marvellous and magnified.

'Underneath?' Humph said. He stretched out his fat soft hand. He had forgotten about his spectacles and started making bubbling noises of excitement.

'Golly, Golly,' he kept saying and then suddenly he was slipping, slowly and fatly, down the bank and then, slowly and fatly, into the water.

'That's because I hadn't got my glasses. That's because I hadn't got my glasses. Where are my glasses? Give me my glasses.'

At first he laughed because Humph looked so queer and soft and undressed without his bike-lamps. Then he thought Humph would start crying and all of a sudden he felt sorry for him and gave him back the glasses. In the end he always felt sorry for Humph. Nobody else did. Everybody teased Humph because he was fat and soft and couldn't see. At the same time everybody said how clever Humph was and what books he read and what a lot he knew.

Somehow he trusted Humph. Somehow all his faith in Humph was restored the moment he put his bike-lamps on.

As they went on it was hot in the little valley. It was August and there was a thundery breath among the brown-silver, turning heads of reed. He and Humph got thirsty and knelt down by the spring and cupped their hands and drank the cold, fresh, spurting water.

'Not too much,' Humph said. 'You don't have to drink too much when you climb mountains. It gives you belly-ache.'

That was an example of the sort of clever things Humph knew.

And then suddenly, from the crest of the field, above the reeds, they saw in the distance a marvellous thing. At least Humph saw it first, and then he did too.

'Mountains!' Humph said. 'Mountains!'

Humph began dancing up and down, so that the fleshy part of his face, under his white ears, waggled up and down like a hen's gills.

'Mountains! Mountains! Look how blue they are. Mountains!'

At first he knew quite well that the great dark blue colander domed above the fields in the east was a cloud; he thought he saw it grow larger and higher, thunder-wise, even as he stared at it. Then Humph said:

'Here, you have the bike-lamps. Look at it through the bike-lamps.'

When he put on the bike-lamps the cloud seemed to go much farther away and was blurred. It changed and was softer. The shape of it was not so much like a colander as a shock of wheat in a field. It really looked in some way like a big, lead-coloured, brooding mountain.

'I told you, I told you,' Humph said. 'I told you there'd be mountains.'

'Can you see it without your specs?'

'No,' Humph said, 'but I know it's there.'

He gave Humph his spectacles back. The big blobs of glass danced fatly in that way that always made him feel sorry for Humph. And then because he did not want to hurt Humph by saying that the mountain was only a cloud he began pretending to believe that it was a mountain. He actually wanted it to be a mountain. He wanted it to be there as much as Humph did.

'Come on,' Humph said. 'We've got to start marching. We've got to get there before night-time.'

Then they were in strange country. They climbed the last of the fences in the fields he knew. They were far from home and he was aware, on the new, high ground, of a sense of exultation. They were explorers, men in a strange land, alone and excited, brave and seeking something.

All the time it seemed to grow hotter. Part of the distances of wheat and barley and grass were shrouded in the day-time duskiness of thunder. On others a queer white light lay stark and brilliant, so that the fields of barley were a mass of flat still flame.

Then, many fields further on, they were out on a road.

He was disappointed about that. His illusion that they were men in some wild uncivilized place vanished suddenly. Then from the mountainous mass of cloud across the corn-fields there came the first stunning bark of thunder. He saw the cloud actually lift itself like a column of unfurling purple smoke in the sky. He knew that at any moment it would rain from across these sultry burning fields but Humph thought different:

'That's the gods,' he said. 'They always talk on mountains. You have to give them offerings. If you don't they growl like that.'

'We ought to get shelter.'

'Not under a tree though,' Humph said. 'Else we'll be struck.'

He had a terrible fear of being struck. He saw a yellow snake of lightning wriggle all the way down the darkening cloud. Another bark of thunder came from a whole pack of dogs charging overhead. He felt a hot fat spot of rain on his face and at the same time a voice shouted:

'Here! You better git in here along o' me if you don't want to git drownded.'

Then they were sitting under the big umbrella of a sloe-hedge, with a man. He was a man in a thousand. One of his eyes had a queer solid glassy look, like a marble, and it did not move when the other did. By his side was a sickle, with a white whetstone, and a straw labourer's bag. He was drinking something golden-tawny from a bottle. On a doorstep of bread he had a piece of red cheese as thick as a book and on top of the cheese an onion as large as a turnip. He cut at all this with a horn-handled shut-knife. Every time he put the knife to his mouth he turned it over at the last moment, and then sucked in bread and cheese and onion with a great smacking, slithering sound.

'Here it comes,' he said. 'Send it down, David.'

He had a sack on his shoulders. His trousers were tied below the knees with string. His boots had great steel strips on the heels and all over the soles.

Rain came hissing down in solid summer sheets and he said:

'Here, you git underneath this here sack along o' me. You won't hurt then. There's room a-new for the three on us under here.'

The storm strode across the land in unaccountably swift black strides. The road, baked from the heat of noon, steamed under rain. Sun was already shining on the distances where the mountain had been and presently the man said:

'It'll all be over in two shakes. Where do you boys come from?'

They told him.

'Well, that ain't far. You ain't got far to go.'

That was disappointing. Humph had said once that he reckoned they had come at least twelve miles, reckoning four miles to the brook and half a mile for every field; and most of the time, especially when the mountain was in view, it seemed like that.

But what happened next was not disappointing.

'That's a rare pair o' specs you got there, boy,' he said. 'One o' these days I'm goin' to git myself a pair like that.'

'You can try them on if you like,' Humph said.

He took off the spectacles and huffed on them and polished them on his coat sleeve.

'Very like ain't my size,' the man said.

'You try them. Humph lets everybody try them.'

The man put on the spectacles. They were much too small for him. They always looked so large on Humph but now they looked no bigger than glassy pennies. But with them perched on his nose the man looked very funny and Humph and himself laughed at the way he stared down through the thick white lenses.

'No,' he said, 'they ain't much good to me.'

He took the spectacles off and gave them back to Humph.

'You see,' he said, 'I ain't only got but this 'ere one eye.'

'No?' they said.

'No,' he said.

All of a sudden he did a remarkable thing.

'There,' he said.

In the palm of his hand lay a naked eye-ball.

'You mean you can take your eye out?' Humph said.

'This 'ere one I can,' he said. 'Tek it out of a morning and wash it. And tek it out of a night when I go to bed.'

Where the eye had been was only a red blood-shot slit. In his hand the glass eye looked exactly like a wet bull's-eye that you had sucked a few times and taken out of your mouth to see if the colour had changed.

'Out she comes,' he said, 'and in she pops again.'

In a flash of a second the eye was back in its socket, glassily staring at the slackening rain.

'Doesn't it hurt when you take it out?'

'No.'

'Did it hurt when you lost it?'

'Like pepper and salt it did.'

'How did you lose it?'

'Shot,' the man said. 'Shot out.'

'In a battle?'

'In a battle,' he said. 'Spion Kop.'

'Where's Spion Kop?'

'Africa,' he said. 'It's a sort of mountain.'

He thought that that was a wonderful thing, and he felt he had to ask a question.

'Does everything look different with only one eye?' he said. 'It looks different when you put Humph's glasses on.'

'Well, very like it does,' he said. 'Only I can't recollect now what it looked like wi' two.'

'I wouldn't like to have only one eye.'

'You wouldn't?' he said. 'Well, I'll tell you summat.'

'What?'

'You only got one eye to see with,' he said. 'But then you only got one eye to tune with. When you got summat to cry about you only want half the quantity o' tears.'

Both he and Humph thought that was very funny.

'And that's a very useful thing,' he said, 'when you're a-ettin' onions.'

They thought that was very funny too. By that time the rain had stopped altogether. The road was steaming in brilliant sunshine. All the grasses of the roadside and the leaves of the hedgerows and the ears of corn were dancing with beads of water.

'If you step out sharp,' the man said, 'you'll git home be dinner-time. So long.'

'So long,' they said.

As they walked home all the fields of wheat and barley

dried in the sunshine until they were fiery and brilliant again under rain. The cloud that Humph had said was a mountain had rolled away and the sky was pure with summer.

That was a wonderful day; he never forgot that day. To find a man with only one eye to cry with was a marvellous thing.

Better even than finding the source of the world.

The Poison Ladies

WHEN you are only four, seven is a hundred and five inches are a mile.

Ben was seven and I was four and there were five inches between us. Ben also had big brown leather patches on the seat of his moley corduroy trousers and dark hairs on his legs and a horn-handled knife with two blades, a cork-screw and a thing he called a stabber.

'Arter we git through the fence,' Ben said, 'we skive round the sloe bushes and under them ash trees and then we're in the lane and arter that there's millions and millions o' poison berries. Don't you eat no poison berries, will you? else you'll die. I swallered a lot o' poison berries once and I was dead all one night arter-wards.'

'Real dead?'

'Real dead,' Ben said. 'All one night.'

'What does it feel like to be dead?'

'Fust you git terrible belly ache,' Ben said, 'and then your head keeps going jimmity – jimmity – jimmity – bonk – bonk – bonk – clang – bang – jimmity – bonk – clang – bonk all the time.'

'Does it make you sick?'

'Sicking up all the time,' Ben said, 'and seeing old men dancing upside down on the bedroom wall and laughing at you – like my Uncle Perce does when he comes home from The Unicorn.'

'I don't want to be dead,' I said, 'I don't want to be dead.'

'Then don't eat no poison berries. You know what poison berries look like, don't you?'

'No.'

'Some are red,' Ben said, 'and some are black. But all on 'em make you sick and give you belly ache and make your head jimmity – jimmity – bonk – clang – bonk – bang – jimmity –'

My blood felt cold. I felt like sobbing and above me, where I lay face downwards under the blackberry hedge, giant stalks of cow parsnip stood like bone-white skeleton sentinels against the late summer sky.

'Why don't we start?' I said. I knew we had a long way to go; Ben said so.

Ben got his knife out and opened the stabber.

'I got to see if there's any spies fust,' Ben said. 'You stop here.'

'How long?'

'Till I git back,' Ben said. 'Don't you move and don't you shout and don't you show yourself and don't you eat no poison berries.'

'No,' I said. 'No.'

Ben flashed the knife so that the stabber pierced the blackberry shade.

'You know Ossy Turner?' he said.

'Yes,' I said. 'Yes.'

Ossy had a hare-lip and walked with one drawling foot and a crooked hand. I always felt awfully sorry for Ossy but Ben said:

'Ossy's like that because he come down here and dint

look for spies fust – so they got him and done that to him.'

'Who did?'

Ben was crawling away on hairy knees, flashing the stabber in the sunlight, leaving me alone.

' "The Poison Ladies",' Ben said, 'what live down here. In that house I told you about. Them two old wimmin what we're goin' to see if we can see.'

Ben went crawling forward; the brown leather patches on his trousers seat vanished clean from my range of sight. I shut my eyes and lay down alone in dead blackberry leaves and tried to listen for skylarks singing. Whenever I was alone in the fields I listened for the sound of skylarks. The song always seemed to sparkle in the solitude.

But now it was nearly September. It was too late for skylarks and all I could hear was the simmering drone of grasshoppers among yellowing grasses, out in the sun.

It was fifty years before Ben came back. I knew quite well that it was fifty years; I counted every one of them.

'No footmarks,' Ben said.

'I didn't eat any poison berries. I didn't –'

'Let's have a look at your tongue!'

My tongue shot out like a frightened lizard. With big white eyes Ben glared down my throat and said:

'All right. We're going now. Hold your breath.'

'How far is it now?'

'Miles,' Ben said. 'Down the lane and past the shippen and over the brook and then up the lane and across the Akky Duck.'

I didn't know what the Akky Duck was; I thought it must be a bird.

'It's like bridges,' Ben said. 'It's dark underneath. It's where the water goes over.'

'Do the poison ladies live there?'

'They come jist arterwards,' Ben said. 'We hide under the Akky Duck and arter that you can see 'em squintin' through the winders.'

The veins about my heart tied themselves in knots as I followed Ben out of the blackberry shade, over the fence, into the lane and past black bushes of sloe powderily bloomed with blue fruit in the sun.

Once I tried to draw level with Ben and walk beside him, just for company, but he turned the stabber on me sharply and said:

'You keep behind me. I'm leader. I know the way, see? I got to git there fust to see if it's all right, see? Else they might do to you what they did to old Ossy, see?'

'Yes, Ben. Yes, Ben. Yes, Ben. Yes, Ben.'

Not long after that we passed a place in the brook where sheep were washed. Ben said I was to look at the water and see how gold it was. That was because it was poison and you'd die if you washed your hands there. Just beyond it great elephant umbrellas of hemlock grew in lush wet shade and Ben said they were poison too.

'Keep in,' he kept saying. 'Keep in. Crouch down. We're coming to the Akky Duck.'

Soon we were crouching under the dark bricks of the bridge. It was suddenly cold and the bricks dripped water. Ferns sprouted green fingers from crevices and Ben said there were snails as big as turnips there, with horns as long as bike-pumps.

'And snakes. And lizards. And rats. And Devil's Coach and Horses.'

'Are they poison too?'

'All on 'em. Everythink's poison down here.'

I wanted to hang on to Ben's coat tails and play horses, but Ben said no, he was going on ahead again to look for spies and that I'd got to wait and stand still and not breathe a word until he whistled a signal back to me.

So I stood under the Akky Duck all alone while Ben went out into the sunlight at the far end to look for spies. I didn't see any snails or lizards or snakes or Devil's Coach and Horses, but water dripped about me in long slow spits, splashing in the shadow.

When Ben whistled at last I jumped clean out of my skin and started running through black pools of water.

'Don't run, you wet ha'puth,' Ben said. 'They'll hear you. They got ears like old sows. They hang down to their shoulders.'

I think I must have shivered as I came out into sunlight, because Ben said:

'You ain't frit, are you?'

'No,' I said. 'No. I'm not frit.'

'If you're frit,' Ben said. 'they'll *know*. Then they'll put both on us in the copper.'

'Why?' I said. 'Why?'

'To boil us up, you wet ha'puth!' Ben said. '*To boil us up*.'

'You said once they poisoned you.'

'So they do,' Ben said. 'Poison you fust, then boil you arterwards.'

Before I could speak again Ben was pointing ahead.

'There it is. That's where they live,' he said. 'That's the house.'

Fifty yards ahead stood a double-bayed house of red brick with a blue slate roof and cowls with foxes' tails on the chimneys. The cowls were black. Half the slates were off the roof and most of the glass was broken in the windows.

When we got a little nearer I could see there were plum trees in the garden, with ripe blue oval fruit shining in the sun. I could see an empty chicken run overgrown with grass and a big red earthenware pot with huge rhubarb leaves growing out of the top like inside-out umbrellas. It was hot now after the tunnel and everywhere the grass-hoppers whirred.

I started to say that the house was empty but Ben said:

'Ah! That's what *you* think. That's what the old wim-men *want* you to think.'

'Why do they?'

'They want you to climb the fence and start gittin' the plums and then jist as you're gittin' 'em they spring out an' collar you.'

The veins about my heart tied themselves into tighter, colder knots as we crept along the fence on our hands and knees.

'Crouch down,' Ben kept whispering. 'Crouch down. Don't let 'em see you.'

Then we were in front of the house, in full view of the broken windows, the slateless rafters and the smoky cowls. The sun was on our backs and the light of it sharpened the splintered windows. The plums looked big and luscious now and you could see yellow wasps turning and shimmering madly about the trees.

'The plums are poison anyhow,' Ben said, 'even if they dint collar you. And even if you dint die o' poison the wasps 'd sting you to death.'

All about the house, from the broken window sashes to the stiff black fox tails, there wasn't a single movement in the sun.

Then Ben was clutching my arm and whispering hoarsely and pointing upward.

'There they are. There's one on 'em now. Watching.'

'Where?' I said. 'Where?'

'Up at that window. On the left-hand side.'

Ben didn't know his right hand from his left hand and nor did I. He pointed with the hand he held his knife in and I stared at the right-hand upstairs window but there was nothing there.

'Can't you see her?' Ben said. 'She's got long white pigtails and you can see her big ears.'

I looked at all the windows, one by one, upstairs and down, but there was nothing to be seen except splintered holes in the glass, naked and white-edged in the sunlight.

'She don't have no teeth, this one,' Ben said, 'and her mouth's all green.'

I didn't dare tell Ben I couldn't see anything, but suddenly he grabbed my arm.

'And there's the other one!' he whispered. 'Downstairs. The one with yeller eyes.'

My heart curdled. I started shivering down the whole length of my spine.

'Big yeller eyes she's got,' Ben said. 'Big yeller eyes. Like brimstone.'

All the windows downstairs were empty too and the only yellow I could see was in the clouds of wasps whirling about the laden plum trees.

'Can't you see her?' Ben said. 'Can't you see her?'

'No.'

He turned and looked at me sharply, in derision.

'You'll never see 'em with your eyes wide open like that, you wet ha'porth. You gotta squint with 'em. Squint. Like this, see? Like owls do, see?'

Ben had his eyes all screwed up so that they were no more than dark slits.

'Owls can see in the dark,' he said. 'They can see what ain't there when we look. You know that, don't you?'

I knew that; my father had told me so. And suddenly I screwed up my eyes like an owl's too, just like Ben.

And when I looked at the house again it was just as Ben had said. I too could see the two old women at the windows, one upstairs and one down, the two old poison ladies, one with yellow eyes and the other with a green mouth and long white pigtails, both of them with awful ears, like sows.

'I can see them now, Ben,' I said, 'I can see them now.'

'Look out! They're coming!' Ben said. 'They're arter us!'

Then we were running, in terror, faster than wasps, under the Akky Duck, past the hemlock, the gold poison water, the shippen and the blue-black aisles of sloes. My breath was burning my chest and throat but my spine was chilled from the hairs of my neck downward and the knots round my heart coiled more and more tightly, deadly cold.

We didn't stop running until we were out in the big open field at the top of the lane. Then Ben started laughing and I was laughing too.

'We seen 'em!' Ben said. 'Both on 'em! They was there! We seen 'em! They was there!'

'We seen 'em!' I said. 'We seen 'em!'

Ben began turning somersaults in the grass and I tried to turn somersaults too. All the time we were laughing and flinging up our hands and shouting.

'I could see her yeller eyes!'

'And the other one's green mouth!'

'And the white pigtails!'

'And their big ears!'

Suddenly a rook cackled sharply in the meadows below us, down where the hemlock grew. Ben looked back down the lane, startled, and I was startled too.

'Let's play horses,' Ben said. 'Let's gallop all the way home.'

'I'll be horse,' I said and in a second I was out in front, champing my bit, with Ben holding my coat tails, and a moment later we were away like a cold thin wind.

'We see the poison ladies!' Ben kept shouting. 'We see the ole poison ladies!'

'We see the poison ladies!' I echoed. 'We see the old poison ladies!'

'They chased us! They nearly got us!'

'They nearly got us!'

'I bet they don't cut their ole nails fer a million years.'

'I bet they don't cut their old nails for a million years.'

Everything Ben shouted I shouted too. When he laughed I laughed. What he believed I believed. He wasn't afraid and I wasn't afraid. I was only flying home like a wild wind.

When you are only four, seven is a hundred and five inches are a mile.